MURDER SO FINAL

MUCKRAKER MYSTERY #3

CLIFTON · NELSON

Murder So Final (Muckraker Mystery #3)
Ted Clifton & Stanley Nelson
ISBN 978-1-77342-092-9

Produced by IndieBookLauncher.com
www.IndieBookLauncher.com
Editing: Stanley Nelson
Cover Design: Saul Bottcher
Interior Design and Typesetting: Saul Bottcher

The body text of this book is set in Adobe Caslon.

Also Available
E-book edition, ISBN 978-1-77342-079-0

CONTENTS

PROLOGUE

Tulsa, Oklahoma

A foul smell added to the sense of danger at the big tank farm in Tulsa's oil alley. It was guarded with a zeal usually reserved for the military. Oil companies were secretive by nature, and Connex Petroleum was no exception with its "No Admittance" signs posted all along the vast fences.

"What's goin' on?" Dick Fitzgerald, police beat reporter for the *Tulsa Herald,* asked the crowd. There were mostly TV people gathered there on a humid, cloudy night.

"Not sure," a TV cameraman answered, peering into the dark. "Cops have got everything blocked off. Think there's a body by the river. After all the rain, it's got to be a godawful mess down there." He frowned. "They won't let us set up our lights, so we can't get much."

Some poor bastard tumbled down that slope into the grime, Dick thought, *no doubt dead. And this sonofabitch is worried about his damn TV pictures not being bright enough.* On most days he wasn't proud to be one of the news herd.

"Okay, people, you're going to have to move back," a voice called out. "We need to get a coroner's truck in here. Clear out." That meant one thing: a body.

Dick nodded to the cameraman. "Good guess."

The sloping bank was muddy, and police slipped and slid down to where the body lay near twenty hulking oil storage tanks lined up into the distance. It felt dangerous being so close to them.

"Get out of the way. What is wrong with you fuckin' people?" The man shouting and cussing as he shoved his way through the less-than-obliging throng was the Tulsa police chief, Samuel Jackson, often referred to by the local press as "Sammy the Cop." He'd made threats against the *Herald's* publisher over that nickname, but it stuck.

It started to rain again. Sammy the Cop's expletive-riddled complaints could easily be heard atop the bank.

"Do you think that smell means anything?" asked the only female reporter in attendance. She looked mad as hell because the rain began to fall harder, pasting her hair to her scalp.

"These tank farms smell that way. Don't think it's dangerous. Of course, if I'm wrong, we probably won't know about it," another wiseass cameraman spoke up, thinking he sounded clever. He didn't.

The next remark came from the well-known political reporter for the Tulsa paper, Mathew Tomas, who'd just arrived. "I wouldn't smoke out here. These grounds are permeated with oil. Might not blow up, but it'll sure as hell burn."

"Hey, Matt. Haven't you written about some kind of fraud involving these tanks?"

Tomas nodded toward the voice in the dark. "Always nice to meet a reader. Was that Sammy I heard going down there?"

"Yep. Bet it feels real familiar." The wiseass cameraman was going to keep at it until he found a line that got a laugh.

Tomas had a bad feeling. He'd been to this tank farm before, when he was run off by security guards and told to stay away or they'd beat the shit out of him. More than a year before that, he received an insider tip that Connex was using the tank farm and others around oil country to defraud investors.

He'd been working on getting evidence and documentation to support that ever since, with little luck. He'd written about allegations that Connex claimed empty tanks in its Louisiana farms were full so the company could borrow millions. But he still had nothing concrete.

Policemen tugged a tarp-covered body up the muddy slope, yelling at each other to be more careful. The guy they hauled up was beyond caring. They slid the load into the panel truck.

The chief stalked up to the crowd. "Don't know why the hell you're hanging around. Yes, we have a body. Don't know who. Once we do, we'll have to notify next of kin. Then, and only then, we might tell you vultures. At this point we have nothing to say, and we want you to clear out. So get the hell out of here." The chief made friends wherever he went. The chances of him being referred to as "Sammy the Cop" went up again.

Tomas hung back, sure the body had to do with the story he'd been chasing. He edged toward one of the coroner's people.

"Anything strange about the body?" he tried to keep his voice casual.

"You know I can't tell you. Sammy the Cop would have me shot."

"Speaking of getting shot—that's what happened, right?"

"You reporters. I'm surprised more of you aren't our customers."

Everybody's a comedian. "If not shot, killed somehow."

The man's voice dropped. "Keep me out of the papers. He was hit in the head. A club or a steel rod. Dead before he hit bottom. Now, beat it."

Murder. But why?

1
MY HOW TIME FLIES

1971. Charles Manson and three of his followers are sentenced with the death penalty for a series of grisly cult-style murders. Walt Disney World opens in central Florida. The *New York Times* publishes the Pentagon Papers, showing the U.S. government had been lying about the Vietnam War, adding to the unpopularity of both. Average U.S. income was $10,600 a year. The average new house cost $25,250.

Oklahoma City, Oklahoma

Tommy Jacks sat in the *OK Journal* newsroom taking a moment of reflection on his brief career thus far as a newspaper columnist. There'd been big, important events and many little, insignificant ones. Somehow, they all seemed to blend in his thoughts, like one stream of life, good and bad, all mixed together.

He was smarter and wiser than when he first stepped out of journalism school into the real world. He'd become aware of his limits and what he still needed to learn about life. The gut-wrenching loss of his first love was an experience that influenced how he thought and felt. Still, each day it moved further into the past.

"You goin' to that symposium downtown?" inquired Vince Young, a friend and fellow writer at the *Journal.*

"I guess. Fred made it sound like a big deal because the paper's paying for it." He meant Fred Simpson, their city editor. "Know what it's about?"

"Supposed to be a discussion about the future of the news business. Main speaker is Doctor Howard Fillmore, president of Corinthian Oklahoma College out by Enid. He's written a lot about us, like how most of us should be doing something more useful like garbage collection."

"Interesting. So newspapers are sponsoring a symposium on how bad we are?"

"Yeah. Hope we won't be singled out. There'll be panel discussions, too. Some on newspapers and some about TV. Personally, I'm opting for the TV sessions. At the least, all the women there'll be good-looking." Vince grinned.

It had only been a few years since Tommy graduated from the University of Oklahoma. His work on the school paper established his muckraking approach to reporting and infuriated most of the department heads who had come under his scrutiny. He graduated early with a hearty "good riddance," and embarked on his career with the *OK Journal,* a struggling daily newspaper in Oklahoma City.

Fred was his first boss. Tommy respected him and usually listened to his advice. Still, they viewed much of life through different lenses. Fred was more focused on the survival of the paper. Tommy was more about slaying invisible dragons. That naturally led to some conflicts. Fred generally won.

After only a few months, Tommy was asked to restart "My

View," a column once written by Taylor Albright. Tommy knew him, and he was a friend of his father's, but that didn't keep him from feeling reluctant to step into the troubling history associated with Albright and the column. But the request came from Bill Anderson, the paper's founder. So he took on the challenge and became the paper's most talked-about opinion writer, young as he was.

His focus was politics, although intrigue and even murder got mixed into the overflowing vat of stories about people, conflicts, and gossip. Tommy developed a local and then a national reputation for meeting every challenge head-on. He was still young and of quiet demeanor, but his columns were direct and hard-hitting. Seldom did he pull a punch. He became a favorite of the newspaper's every-day readers, but was not appreciated so much by the power elite.

"Need a ride downtown?" Vince seemed eager to see what was going on at the symposium.

"Nah. Think I'll drive in case I want to leave early."

The symposium was sponsored by the Oklahoma Press Association, although the *Journal*, the *Tulsa Herald*, and the *Oklahoma Sun* mostly bankrolled it. The *Sun* and the *Journal* competed for the Oklahoma City market and had a bitter history, usually fighting anything the other supported. Their constant head-knocking meant difficult financial times for both. But in a landmark decision, they entered a joint operating agreement and started sharing production, printing, and circulation departments. That wouldn't have been possible without the death of the founder of the *Sun*, J.H. Gilmore. He'd been the driving force behind the dominant paper since the early 1900s. His son, Robbie Gilmore, while still aggressive and opinionated, was a notch or two more reasonable.

The symposium was at the Skirvin Hotel, by far the most opulent building in the city. It was grand by any standard that could be applied, an amazing overstatement in conservative, cautious Oklahoma. It stood as a testament to the gushing exorbitance of the oil industry's gilded age.

Trying not to gawk at the outlandish chandeliers, Tommy found the registration desk. Securing entry entitled him to a bag of free stuff and a name tag. He entered the vast ballroom arranged with a sea of large round tables and a breakfast buffet. After piling on more food than he'd eat, he found a table.

"Hey there, Mister Famous Columnist."

Tommy knew the voice without turning to look. "Hey there yourself, Miss Beautiful TV Hostess."

They hugged. Tracy Jacks, once Tracy Clark, was one of the most important people in his life. He had adopted her as his mom, even if she was only a few years older. Then she married his dad and *became* his mom.

"Here to learn how bad we are?" Tracy demonstrated her movie-star smile.

Tommy chuckled. "If it gets too bad, I might get up and leave."

"Apparently, based on what I hear, Fillmore isn't real keen on our contribution to society." Even if they joked, it was a serious matter that news organizations weren't seen as handling responsibilities many considered key to a successful democracy.

"Yeah," Tommy nodded, "things are all screwed up, with protests, riots, wars, and racism. And who's at fault? Us. Not sure I buy that, but there's no question everything we do is changing. And I'm not real sure it's in good ways."

"I know. I'm here with people from the station, so I better go be sociable. Come see us on Sunday, okay?"

"Yep, it's a Monopoly date." They both smiled. Tracy was a notoriously competitive Monopoly player. Win at your own risk.

A quiet fell over the room as Hank Edwards, president of the OPA, came to the lectern.

"It's an honor," he began, "for me to introduce our speaker today. I have known Doctor Howard Fillmore for many years. Many of you may not know he was a journalism professor at Oklahoma State University. He's been a great friend of mine over a long time. I'm aware that many of you think he's a critic of journalism, but he's not. He's an outspoken critic of *bad* journalism. He can explain what that means. Please welcome Doctor Fillmore."

Fillmore rose to a polite round of applause.

"When Hank asked me to make opening remarks for this symposium," he began, "I was surprised, as no doubt you were when you found out I was the speaker. I've had some harsh things to say about the news business, but they were all meant to be constructive. Our freedoms in this country are based on free speech. One of the most important aspects of free speech is a free press. Guaranteed by the First Amendment, a free press is a unique part of our founding. You, seated at these tables, are part of that guarantee, fought for with lives, defended by great people of all political persuasions. You are the free press that protects our rights in this country. Our founding fathers said it was one of the most important aspects of our democracy. No one at that time could imagine a free press that would not inform the public of what was going on in their government;

no one could have imagined a press that would become so enmeshed with the entertainment business it would abandon its primary role of watchdog. It's a changing world, and I think the collective media have a great responsibility to examine themselves and make sure they understand what these changes mean to our future."

Fillmore went on to describe changes he thought needed to be considered by news organizations. His audience, while perhaps skeptical, was attentive.

"I don't expect everyone in this room to agree with all my ideas," he summed up. "I'd be shocked if you did. All I'm suggesting is that we, as professionals, cannot ignore what is in front of us every day. The news business is becoming something different. And it is up to us to make sure that whatever that ends up being still fulfills the vision given us by the founding fathers of this great country. Thank you."

He was rewarded with something of an ovation. There were yet doubters in the crowd, but Fillmore had come across as a thoughtful man who wanted something better from the news people collected there, and those people more than anyone understood the importance of their role in their country.

The man sitting next to Tommy turned. "Great speech. I worry about all the things he mentioned, especially the corporate control. Seems like there are fewer papers every year."

Tommy nodded. "Not sure what can be done, but it's encouraging that it's being discussed." He extended a hand. "Tommy Jacks, *OK Journal.*"

"How 'bout that? You're one of the people I wanted to look up. Mathew Tomas, *Tulsa Herald.* Call me Matt."

"Well, sure. I've read your stuff. We dig in the same field.

Great to meet you."

"We may dig in the same field, but you write a column. You can give your opinions. My editors are hard-nosed about facts. I skip more shit than I can write about." Tomas's enthusiasm was apparent and contagious.

"Yeah," Tommy chuckled. "A lot of reporters hate me. The column gives me a lot more freedom, but there are demands. For example, you don't have to cover society events, while my editors insist I attend this or that charity ball."

"I'm working on somethin' that's been going on for months," Matt continued, "but I'm not able to get anything into print. If you have time later, I'd sure like to talk about it with you."

"Are you offering to share a lead with me?" Tommy's voice expressed his skepticism.

Matt shrugged. "Well, I don't know. I just met you, but I read your stuff. I've been beating my head against this wall for some time. This story's become important to me—not for my ego, but for the reasons Fillmore was talking about. My responsibility."

"Okay. When and where?"

"There were a couple of panels I wanted to attend, so maybe at around four in the bar? I'm staying here, so most anytime works for me."

"Four sounds good."

Matt leaned closer. "I don't want to oversell you on this, but I think some of what I know is tied to Henry Blackman, owner of Connex and soon to be the Republican candidate for the U.S. Senate." He looked eager to share what he had. About that time, it was announced the first panel was getting ready to start. "Well, need to run. See ya."

"Yeah." Tommy was intrigued. Since he'd become a little better known, lots of people had offered him tidbits that seldom turned out to be anything. He'd meet with him but didn't expect much. He did want to see if he could find Fillmore, maybe to get an interview scheduled with him.

OK Journal

My View—Tommy Jacks

Just a little before my time there was a national television journalist named Edward R. Murrow. He worked during the days when all the sets looked pretty much alike. You could cover the screen with a shop rag, and the pictures were relentlessly black, white, and kind of smudgy.

Murrow wouldn't have gotten away with as much as he did then these days. He smoked about a pack a broadcast, right in front of you. His delivery, as they call it in the TV business, was more a monotone mutter. And he hardly looked into the camera.

But he'd look the powers that were in the eye and make them flinch. He had cast-iron guts. He didn't back down when he was right, which he usually was. He and a crew of other believers in the better promises of American democracy put together a documentary about how America wasn't keeping those promises.

"Harvest of Shame" ruined the Thanksgiving appetites of millions of viewers in 1960. Everyone who saw it had to look down at what they'd just said grace over and couldn't help but realize it all got to their tables because people—truckloads of them—who didn't have nine-to-five jobs were being used like so many shop rags by big-time commercial farmers.

The institution that calls itself journalism these days—as if that word is a semi-proper noun that has to mean something official—never shrinks from the irony of reminding us that "Harvest of Shame" won a Peabody Award for its unflinching honesty. What's meant by that is this: journalism, as an institution, loves to wave its own little flag in remembrance of what's been done in its name because that takes your attention away from what it's not doing anymore.

Sure, the life of a journalist is getting tougher only 11 years after "Harvest of Shame." That's to be expected, in one way, because the longer we're at this, the more people catch on to the idea of what we're trying to do. By that same token, more people get anxious about us following Murrow's footsteps and uncovering the filthy things they're trying to do.

But what no journalist bargained for was getting handcuffed by the places where we work. Sure, every paper, every TV station, every radio station with a news department has "sacred cows." But we're also talking about the stations and papers getting bought out and merged and churned into "news" leviathans that swallow everything in their path with a mindless indifference just to regurgitate it onto your breakfast table. Here's your paper. Tune in at six. Don't miss the top story of the day.

Here's the thing: tips for your garden, the latest avocado casserole recipe from Chicago, and the rest of the bagful of fodder that could only interest the few people who can afford to retain lawyers or see their doctors anytime the mood strikes them, are not news.

Life and death—that's news. That's what journalists are really here for. That's what the big guys are doing their dead level best to keep you from noticing: what they're not really covering.

The guys who sign the paychecks in the fetid bellies of those leviathans want it that way. It makes life easier for them.

And worse, their anoxic strain of journalism spreads even to honest newsrooms that have nothing to do with them. After all, we gotta compete, or so we tell ourselves. That's the sad thing about our business. We're primed to think of ourselves as underdogs for a list of reasons, but these days it's mostly because our circulation numbers are shriveling.

When Murrow would sign off his broadcasts, he'd always say, "Good night. And good luck."

Luck isn't the half of what we need to carve our way out of the belly of this beast.

2
POLITICS AND ODD BEDFELLOWS

"I know your boss." Howard Fillmore seemed most pleased to meet Tommy.

"You mean Fred?" One could hate or like people instantly on first meeting. For Tommy, Fillmore was a "like."

"Well, yes, I know Fred Simpson—he and I go back a long way. But who I meant was Bill Anderson."

Tommy chuckled. "Oh, the *real* boss."

"I also know your father. I spent some time with him during his first days as the state Democratic Party chairman. I was doing a paper on political structure, and he was kind enough to give me some time. So your request for an interview has some precedence. I was totally shocked to hear he'd gone to work for Robbie Gilmore. I guess the J.H. Gilmore days are really over. How's he doing?"

"He and Robbie still don't agree on much, but they've developed a good working relationship." Tommy was almost never comfortable talking about his dad's past, so he changed the subject. He scheduled an interview on the Corinthian campus before Fillmore headed off to find the conference room for his breakout session.

Tommy seriously considered leaving until he spotted his dad. He waved and headed toward him.

"Hoping you'd be here," Tommy said before they hugged. He was always a little surprised by that. His dad was never a hugger until he married Tracy. Now he seemed to hug everyone.

"Well, the paper's helping pay for this, so we've forced a lot of our people to attend. Thought I'd show up, too. Got here a little late, so I stood in the back to hear Fillmore. He's a great speaker. What'd you think?" Ray Jacks was an old-time political operative, and still fairly new to the newspaper business.

"Some of what he said kind of stings. But I'm glad people are thinking about where the news business is headed. He said he knew you."

"Yeah. Ages ago, he tagged along with me for a couple days, back when I was just getting started as state chairman. Seemed like a good guy. You talked to him?"

"I asked him for an interview. We set something up for next week."

"You know; the rumor is Bill's pushing him to be the Democratic candidate for U.S. Senate."

"I had no idea. Why haven't I heard that?"

His dad shrugged. "Since Albright left, you've lost some of your contacts. You need to drop in on Louongo more, get reconnected." Ray Jacks smiled at his son.

Tommy and Taylor Albright used to meet on a regular basis at Denny's on Classen Boulevard. Their sessions were supposedly to read morning papers from across the country, but a lot of local gossip was involved, too. Joe Louongo was a well-known criminal lawyer and an asset to Albright and Tommy's dad in the past.

Still, Tommy had to wonder, "Isn't he a little too far to the left to win a statewide race?"

"That's what I would've said. But there's a lot of push-back against the Republicans for some of the national albatrosses people hang around their necks—Vietnam being a big one. I'm not sure what kind of candidate Fillmore'd make, but I'd think unless he drifted more to the center, he couldn't win here."

"Why would Bill Anderson support him? Seems like there'd be some risk for the *Journal*."

"Probably is, if Fillmore drifted too far left. My guess would be that Bill admires his ethics and honesty. Plus, if it turns out to be Blackman on the Republican side, he'd have no choice but to support a Democrat."

"I've heard of at least three other Democrats who are considering running. Would seem like Fillmore'd be a long shot just to win the primary."

"I don't want to be cynical, but a senate race between Fillmore and Blackman would be an almost perfect match between right and left—liberal and conservative. Would sell a lot of papers."

With genuine surprise in his voice, Tommy asked, "You don't really think Bill's become that cynical, do you?"

"Other people might reach that conclusion, but not me." He gave Tommy an "I'm innocent" look. "Bill will be pleased you're going to interview him. Whether you agree with his politics or not, you'll find Fillmore's a smart guy and not one of the 'I'll cut your taxes and provide more services' types."

They headed to one of the next sessions. Ray was an executive with the *Sun* now, so he couldn't leave and offend one of the sponsors of the event, namely his employer. The session covered the rather mundane but economically critical area of classified ads and how to maximize readership and revenue. It was a little too "nuts-and-bolts" for Tommy, so once it was over he decided to head out and visit his girlfriend.

"Hey, Tommy, what a nice surprise." Patsy was the loveliest person on the planet, at least in Tommy's eyes. "What are you doin' in my neighborhood?" The "neighborhood" was the richly appointed law office of Lawrence Alexander III, one of the top legal minds in the state, and Patsy's uncle.

"There's a newspaper-sponsored event at the Skirvin, and since I was close I thought of you and wanted to see you." Tommy had been asking Patsy to marry him since the first day they became a couple. She kept saying no—not until he was fully grown or became rich, whichever might come first. "How about dinner tonight at Risso's?"

"Pizza, beer, and you. What could be better?" Patsy smiled her wonderful beaming smile.

"I'm meeting with a reporter from the *Tulsa Herald* at four at the Skirvin, but I should be at Risso's by the time you get there from work."

They snuck a hug and kiss. Tommy headed out to see Louongo, on his dad's advice. The office was just a few blocks from the Skirvin in Deep Deuce, once a notorious part of town replete with nightclubs. Some were famous and featured nationally known jazz bands. In the Forties and Fifties, they attracted a racial mix of patrons who appreciated music and an on-the-edge atmosphere. Now the area was turning trendy with new restaurants that lacked authenticity. Louongo's building was one of few that hadn't been torn down or remodeled. It had always stuck out for its grandeur in a once less-than-grand part of the city.

Louongo's door stood open and his office looked empty. "Hello, anyone here?" Tommy asked loudly. No answer. He jotted a note and began to leave.

"What the hell, kid, did you break into my office?" Louongo sounded angry, but Tommy knew he was just being his usual self.

"I was looking for your staff of professionals, but it appears they've all left."

"Glad to see you haven't lost your wiseass sense of humor. To what do I owe the great pleasure of your presence?"

"I missed you." Tommy grinned, but it didn't sell.

"Like hell you did. You in trouble with the cops again?"

"Not yet. What do you know about Howard Fillmore?"

"Ah, political gossip. Looking for dirt for your column? I hear he's going to be the first communist running for the senate from Oklahoma, and the Branchers are going to make sure he loses."

"Branchers? You mean the Freedom Branch Society?"

"Yep. Their main guy in Oklahoma is Thorsten Daniels, and *he hates communists.* Poor old Fillmore won't have any idea what hit him once those fanatics start in." Louongo looked smug to know much juicier political gossip than the kid columnist.

"Never heard of Thorsten Daniels. Where's he been?"

"Probably under a rock. The main push for the Freedom Branch Society is coming out of Kansas. Some nut-job millionaire in Wichita is financing it all around the country. He sent Daniels out here. These guys are so far right they're about to fall off. And if you disagree with them, you're a communist. Fillmore's like catnip to them. They're going to be a factor."

"I thought you only hung out with criminals. How do you know all this?"

"You know; you have a very annoying way about you—are you sure you're Ray Jacks's kid?"

"Okay, sorry. Thanks for the information, Mister Louongo, you are the most knowledgeable person I know. How's that?" Tommy paused to assess Louongo's temperature. "I didn't mean to be rude. I was just curious."

Louongo did not look happy. "I live in the real world, not some journalist's bubble. I talk to people who know shit, they tell me the shit they know because I tell them the shit I know. It's how it works." He looked to be about done with the conversation.

"Okay, I didn't drop by to make you mad. Have you heard anything from Albright since he left?" Tommy really didn't know how to talk to Louongo. Every conversation seemed to end in some kind of huff.

"Nah, he's gone. Understand he's making it big time with his book and doing TV and radio in New York. We won't hear from him again." There was a notable sadness to that remark. Could it be Louongo had feelings?

"Well, take care, Louongo. Maybe we should meet at Denny's sometime, just for old times' sake?"

"Yeah, that'd be great. See ya, kid."

Tommy walked back to his reliable but depressing old car, thinking about how Louongo always seemed to be on edge, ready for a fight. The only time he looked happy was during battle with the system.

The Skirvin's lobby bar was the nicest Tommy had ever been in. He ordered a gin and tonic while he waited, amazed by the price. He could have gotten a chicken-fried steak sandwich, fries, and a Coke at Del Rancho with money left over, for the cost of that drink. Nice bar, but he would only have one, thanks. There weren't a lot of people, which he chalked up to the prices. At one point he thought he saw someone he knew in the bar mirror—someone who made him turn to look. But they weren't there after he turned. He decided he was mistaken. After sipping on his expensive drink for a half hour, he figured Tomas had stood him up. Odd—he'd seemed so eager to talk. Probably something else came up. Tommy stopped at the front desk to have them call Tomas's room to see if maybe he'd decided on a nap and overslept.

"No answer, sir. Would you care to leave a message?"

Tommy scribbled a note with his home phone number and gave it to the clerk. He left with an uncomfortable foreboding he'd experienced in the past, often confirmed by bad things.

"Hey, what's with the hard liquor?" Patsy was a beer-and-pizza girl.

"Had a gin and tonic at the Skirvin and decided to have another because it *has* to be cheaper and just as good." He frowned. "The guy from Tulsa didn't show up. No reason for me to worry, but it felt weird. He had some lead on a story he wanted to talk about, seemed real eager. I just can't understand why he didn't show."

"Do you know him?"

Tommy shook his head. "Just met him, but he seemed okay. He was all excited about some story concerning the oil tank farms he was chasing." He rested his head in his hands. "And there's something else really bothering me." He squirmed. "I was waiting at the bar, and for just a second I thought I saw someone I knew in the mirror. I turned around, but he wasn't there. I think it could've been a guy who used to work at the paper. He disappeared after we found out he'd been involved in some pretty shady stuff."

Patsy frowned and leaned in closer. "What kind of shady stuff?"

"Theft, fraud, drugs, maybe murder."

"Who was that?" Patsy hated the sense of danger that sometimes was part of Tommy's world.

"Chuck Branson." Tommy shuddered just saying the name.

OK Journal

My View— Tommy Jacks

A neat, professionally mixed gin and tonic served in an expertly buffed crystal tumbler over finely sculpted ice and the freshest lime to be had this far from Jamaica would seem just the thing after sitting through a seeing-to by one of our fair state's foremost experts on the journalistic arts.

There's a problem, though. A journalist, especially a foot soldier-gumshoe type like me, doesn't make enough scratch to feel comfortable sipping that gin and tonic in the too-grand-for-this-cowtown bar at the Skirvin. It's not that the joint's out of my league. In this business, you have to be ready and able to discomfit anyone, anywhere, anytime. But in that bar, there's no one within shouting distance, besides the wait staff, who are trained well enough to identify my type on sight, and they steer clear. I wind up having to take a drink like that by thirty-cent sips, at timed intervals, just to get my money's worth. Thereby a good part of an afternoon, not to mention my wallet, are going to waste.

It might have been a good thing the contact who'd promised on his grandmother's life that he would be in the same bar on time didn't show or answer the phone in his room somewhere up the baroque elevator shaft, maybe close enough to touch the darkening floors of the thunderheads flexing their ominous intentions for the evening. If he'd joined me, it might have been necessary to compel him to carve a similarly cavernous hole in his paycheck, too. Misery plus expensive alcohol demands company, and turns dangerously gloomy when it can't get no satisfaction.

And there's a lot more going on guaranteed to darken the soul than a mixed grog at a gut-punch price and the throbbing sting after a fresh scourging suffered in company with journalists gathered to listen to Howard Fillmore, esteemed professor. We've covered that territory. Now, with fetid muck fresh on our boots, it's onward and downward, to rake into the pits of Oklahoma politics.

Rick Butler, the amazing disappearing governor-turned-senator who's occupying Bruce Knight's seat after Knight killed a murderous, heroin-dealing quack and then himself some time ago, is in formation to punt his seat. Already a crowd is gathering to leap and claw for the ball, and devil take the hindmost. I can't tell you how I know this, but Fillmore, a genuinely decent and intelligent man who finds no peer among politicians in this state because he *is* decent and intelligent, is mentioned as a possible first-round pick for all-the-way return man.

The scene is anxiety-inducing, like watching the blue-chip freshman out there on his first play, hoping this kid can break the game open because this game badly needs breaking. Fillmore, or someone even reasonably like him, is what this oil-corn-and-cow state, let alone a country mewling in Nixon's suffocating grip, needs just to get off the floor. But we all know in the dank pits of our hearts he's going to get creamed. The odds against him are too great, and getting greater.

The GOP is bringing in their special teamers and, according to another source who's seriously bad business to betray, they're ringers from Kansas. A clutch of stone-brained Freedom Branch Society mouth-foamers, all locked, loaded and salivating for serious contact sport, is on its way. They're worse than professionals. They're certifiable, committed and as predictable as maddened hornets. The quote to describe them politically was, "These guys are so far right, they're about to fall off the table," and take our fair state with them, presumably. That seems to be their plan.

Maybe Fillmore should stay in the locker room or better yet, exit the stadium. Meanwhile, this gin and tonic is only half gone. And there'll be no refill. Not at these prices. Next meeting's at Del Rancho, and dinner's on me. I promise, it's cheaper than renting a table at the Skirvin.

3

BOOM AND BUST

Henry Blackman had just hung up the phone and was frowning at the vile instrument when his head of security, Ed Black, entered his office.

"Mornin', Henry."

"Just got off the phone with that weirdo Thorsten Daniels—that Freedom Brancher. Says somebody he knows at police headquarters told him they found a body out by one of our tank farms. Said the guy'd had his head bashed in. Wiseass Daniels said the guy worked for the oil commission, and his job was to inspect the tanks. Bastard seemed to suggest maybe we had something to do with it. Did we?"

Ed grew cautious. He'd worked for Henry long before either became a respectable member of the upper crust. They had teamed up when Henry would have been the first person the cops would look for if they found a body with its head busted. "I don't know nothin' about no body out by any of our tanks. Whereabouts was it at?"

Henry glared at his long-time henchman. "You've got connections with the police. Call and find out what the hell's going on. This better not turn out to be anything that'll cause me any problems."

More and more conversations with Henry, once his pal,

happened in threatening tones. Ed had taken care of more shit for Henry than he could remember. He knew Henry when they were the lowest oilfield scum, working on rigs for slave wages. But there'd always been something different about Henry—something a little scary. Ed still feared him. He did as he was told.

Blackman dialed the phone.

"Hillman, Drake, and Matthews, how may I assist you?" The sexy voice said.

"Hey, sweetheart, this is Henry Blackman. Let me talk to Gary." Blackman thought he would give up about half of his fortune to have sex with his attorney's receptionist. *Well maybe not half, but a lot.* He chuckled to himself.

"Morning, Henry."

"When will we get that new stock issue done?" Gary Hillman had been the company's attorney for eight years and was considered one of the best legal minds in Tulsa, especially when it came to the oil industry. Henry knew Gary didn't like him much, but that didn't matter a hell of lot. He always hired the best professionals he could find and treated them like dirt. It made him feel good.

"Should have all the final paperwork ready within a couple of days. I think we can then proceed with the offering. So, maybe two weeks or so from now." Gary's tone suggested he found talking to Henry difficult.

"Can we speed that up?"

"Not much. We don't want to change our announced schedule. That could make investors nervous."

"Thought we were one hundred percent subscribed."

"We are, Henry. But those subscriptions are more like

promises to buy the stock. They're not guaranteed."

Henry spat. "Well, fuck, I'm ready to get this done. Feels like we're just waiting on something to happen to screw this up. We ought to just move forward—we've got plenty of people who want to buy this shit. So let's just do it."

Gary sighed. "As I've told you, Henry, some of the time delays are based on requirements by the regulators. We have to allow certain time periods before we can move on to the next step. I really don't see the problem. We're right on track, and we'll have everything done in a couple of weeks."

"Well, yeah, you just do it your way. It's my goddamn company, my goddamn money, but no, don't listen to me—just do whatever in the fuck you want to. Great. Gotta go." He hung up.

Jeez. A dead tank inspector on their property. What would that news do to his plans? He wasn't sure he could even trust his old pal Ed anymore. The more money and power he had, the less control, it seemed. Everything he did anymore needed someone else's approval. When he started out, he didn't ask anybody's permission for anything. Now here he was, about to run for the U.S. Senate, *which was just madness.* How did he get talked into it? He knew he was still the same hard-edged guy as when he was a roustabout without a nickel in his pocket. But he sure never took any shit off anybody then. Now he had to wait around for other people to get things done. He hated it.

And he was almost broke. How the hell did that happen? Connex was one of the most successful oil companies in Oklahoma. People said he was worth millions, but he and a few others knew the truth. Without this new stock offering, he could be penniless in a few months, all because he pushed his geologists to move into that new field. Every one of those assholes told him they didn't think it was a good play. He hated to be told he couldn't do anything, so he fired them all and replaced them with new people who provided hearty approvals to his plans. It was a massive bust. Connex lost millions in a hurry. They pulled every accounting trick they knew to cover up the massive losses, and here he was, smiling during meetings with donors and talking to the movers and shakers because he was running for the Senate. Representing the people—man, that was a laugh. He didn't give a shit about the people. He knew he should just drop out. But his ego wouldn't let that happen.

"It was just off of Thirty-Third out on the west side, out by the river. Isn't that one of your tank farms? Don't you know where *that* is, Ed?" The cop gave Ed a stupid grin, like he thought he was being clever.

Ed snorted. "I'm just makin' sure where it was. *You* guys didn't contact us, but we did get a tip about something on one of our tank farms, and it's my job to check it out, okay?" He'd dealt with this guy for years, and he seemed to get dumber every year.

The police clerk referred to his paperwork. "Name was Buck Howard. Worked for the state. Guess his job was tank inspection. Maybe he found something wrong, and Connex killed him. Whattaya think, Ed?"

"Very funny. Those guys don't need our permission to be out there, and we had nothing to do with him dyin'. I figure he fell or something. You sure it was murder?"

The clerk went back to his file. "No autopsy yet. Looks like he was hit in the head with some heavy metal object that split his head open—died instantly. Maybe he fell and hit something, but the working hypothesis for now is murder. I'm sure you'll be getting a visit from the detectives anytime now."

Ed drove out to the tank farm. He knew he wouldn't find anything new there, but decided it was better to stay away from Henry. It was one of the smelliest he'd been around, where oil visibly leached into the ground and into the river. In any other state, the place would be condemned and the owners fined untold amounts for clean-up. But Oklahoma was more akin to a support provider for the oil industry than a normal government. What was good for the oil industry was good for Oklahoma, at least in the short term.

"Bud, what the hell's this rumor about you meeting with some yahoos thinking about running against me in the GOP primary? Hope there's nothing to that." Henry enjoyed unobstructed access to the governor based on his huge donations to Evans's campaign.

"Henry, of course that's not true. Just somebody making shit up. Probably some reporter. I fully support your candidacy, and you know it." It amazed Bud Evans how many people he had to suck up to in a typical day.

"It'd better not be true."

Evans clearly heard and grimaced at the threat from one of the richest and best-known assholes in the state.

Blackman continued, "I've got big problems with some of your underlings who run those regulatory commissions. I expect this kind of bullshit from the feds, but from the state government? What the hell's going on? Did everybody suddenly forget where those salaries come from?"

"Listen, Henry. Some of those guys get a little zealous, but we're getting lots of complaints about oil leaks—a lot of 'em—coming from the tank farms. We've got to be smart here. Can't just fire the bastards, or we'll invite the feds in. I've been working with Jefferson over at the Corporation Commission, and he's a reasonable guy. But we need to be smart. Just give me some time, and we'll get this all under control."

Henry fumed, "Well, I don't know what that means, 'be smart.' What I need is these assholes off my back. We're moving oil through Cushing, and that means millions to the state. You want us to go somewhere else—maybe Texas or Louisiana? They'll welcome us with open arms."

Evans rolled his eyes. The threat was nonsense. The tanks and pipelines were where they were because of the oilfields, not out of any sense of obligation to Oklahoma, and they weren't going anywhere. Plus, he knew of hundreds of violations by Connex, not only of laws and regulations but of just good old common sense. They spilled about a third of their damned oil every year, usually close to a river. Evans was no tree-hugging environmentalist, but he wasn't comfortable with dimwitted oil goons like Blackman, either. They seemed to think they could pollute anywhere they wanted. "Henry, just stay calm. I'll talk to the people over at the commission. If I have to, I'll knock some heads. But don't get them all riled up. It'll be better if we try to accommodate some of their more reasonable requests."

"Reasonable, my ass. I want them to stay out of my business. Once I'm elected, I'll start to get this anti-business shit cleaned up for good." Blackman abruptly hung up, not unusual for him.

Evans thought about calling someone at the oil and gas division of the Corporate Commission, but he suddenly tired of the entire mess. When he'd been pro tempore of the state Senate, Bud Evans wielded a lot of power, although he was rarely in the spotlight. Therefore, he did not catch constant flak from lobbyists, interest groups, or other politicians. He'd decided to run for governor to replace Butler at the insistence of his wife, who had twice his ambition. He now seemed to spend most of his day under attack from one misguided group after another. He missed his old job. He wondered if he'd made a mistake.

Following a respectful period of mourning after Senator Bruce Knight shot himself in 1969, Rick Butler, the governor at the time, appointed himself to serve the remainder of Knight's term in the U.S Senate. Democrats cried political foul, but he was in, and they were not. Butler had only one goal: to maximize his retirement. Being a U.S. Senator, even a never-elected one, for two-plus years meant an amazing pension. He was sick and tired of politics. He just wanted to cash out.

Much of his political career had been as a figurehead. Even while governor, as long as J.H. Gilmore was alive, he only did as he was told. After Gilmore's death, people like Henry Blackman became a new and troublesome burden, and now Blackman was calling him several times over the past weeks. Of course, he wanted to make sure Butler would endorse him in the upcoming primaries for the Senate seat he'd be vacating. If he'd had any pride left, he would've told Blackman to go to hell, that he'd endorse anyone other than him, even that Democrat Fillmore. But he was afraid. He'd spent his whole life afraid of someone finding out he didn't know what he was doing. Now it seemed more and more that people thought they should be able to talk to their representatives and actually get answers, and answers were not among his strong points. He'd purchased a small ranch out by Guymon and was looking forward to doing nothing and never talking to loud and pushy people like Henry Blackman again.

4

GOOD NEWS AND BAD NEWS

Tommy called the *Tulsa Herald,* even if it was Saturday, to leave a message for Mathew Tomas. He didn't know Tomas and considered that maybe missing appointments was normal for him. But he had a bad feeling and couldn't shake it. According to the Skirvin, he was still registered. But he didn't answer his phone.

His routine most days was to head to the state capitol press room, a comforting mess of a place littered with desks, phones, and typewriters. He was usually its lone occupant. After he began to write columns more often, he also set up a workspace in his cramped and notoriously untidy apartment, mostly for weekends. Perhaps as a result he'd become better at staying ahead of deadline, which meant fewer panicked calls from June, the assistant city editor, demanding something to print right then.

The focus of his "My View" column was politics, which covered about anything you wanted to bring into the mix. At first, he wrote about state politicians and local gossip, but soon he covered a little more national politics and, of course, whatever gossip he came by. He knew the U.S. Senate race would be a major story over the next several months. That meant he would have to learn more about the candidates, especially the ones who more than likely weren't going to survive past the primaries. Even if such candidates were on the fringes, they were great material. Also, he needed to find out more about the Freedom Branch Society. He'd heard about them and their national campaigns against a handful of real and more often imagined communists, but didn't know enough to feel comfortable writing about them. He headed to one of his favorite places to learn: the library.

His preference was a branch location just off the Northwest Highway, although he could have gone downtown where there was more reference material. But the main one felt huge and unfriendly compared to the branch.

He settled into a small table and began reading. The Branchers, he gathered, were considered extreme right on the political spectrum, an assessment emphasized by their smear campaign against the center-right Republican President Dwight Eisenhower. They claimed, without offering any accountable proof, that Eisenhower was a tool of communists. To defend that reasoning, they insisted the U.S. government was controlled by internationalists, greedy bankers, and corrupt politicians. *No doubt some truth buried somewhere in that,* Tommy thought. The Branchers claimed the goal of internationalists, whom they never identified, was to use the United Nations to form a one-world, socialist government called a "New World Order."

One of the Branchers' primary causes was civil rights. They were opposed to every one of them, and suggested all civil rights organizations, including and especially the American Civil Liberties Union, were controlled by communists. Tommy couldn't imagine living in the dark and ugly world the Branchers occupied, where almost everyone was an enemy.

He discovered interesting material about how the Branchers were structured around strong state organizations. The individual members of the state groups were usually kept secret. They stated in some of their materials that it had to be secret to keep the government and the communists from attacking them and their leaders.

Then he ran across Thorsten Daniels's name. Daniels was a dentist from Sapulpa and had been arrested in Tulsa during an anti-United Nations rally. He was quoted in the *Tulsa Herald* as saying, "We lost many good men fighting those communist (expletives) in Korea and Vietnam, and now Justice Warren and the United Nations is handing our country over to these godless devils." *Yep*, Tommy thought, *that was a good quote. A little strange, but good.* He made a note to get an interview with Daniels.

Tracy walked into the kitchen, stopped and stared. It was fantastic. She'd never lived in such an expensive house. She still felt like she was intruding in someone else's home. She'd lived for years in the small, modest house she bought just after graduating from college. Even when things were good financially, she'd stayed there because the house and neighborhood were comfortable. While she made some effort to project a glamorous image for her television career, she preferred a simpler, plainer world at home. When Ray moved in before they got married, he seemed to enjoy it, too.

Soon after they married, Tracy became the host of a morning TV talk show and an immediate success. The station, fearing she might bolt to a competitor, gave her a big raise and a new contract. She'd never made that kind of money before. And Ray took a job with his old nemesis Robbie Gilmore as a vice president at the largest newspaper, publishing, and broadcast company in the state. They were making money neither of them could have imagined before. In one of those "why not?" moments, they bought and moved into a small mansion in Nichols Hills. "Small mansion"—the words didn't even make sense. But that was how the realtor described it.

"I can't believe we live here." Ray stood behind Tracy, admiring the same fantastic kitchen.

"I know. It seems weird, like we're trespassing or something." Tracy giggled and smiled at Ray. They hugged for a long time.

"Well, why not? I'm an executive and you're a TV star. It's our right, as privileged people." Ray puffed out his chest. Tracy took a good swing and hit him in the shoulder. He complained about her strength, and they laughed at and with each other.

"You know," she sighed, looking around again, "Tommy's coming over tomorrow. I wonder what he's going to think."

"Yeah," Ray nodded, "he'll either think we've turned into plutocrats and start to shun us, or he'll want to move in—if we hire a maid."

They hugged and laughed again. Like most normal people who'd stumbled into good fortune, they were nervous that something bad would happen next, because it usually did.

"Hey, Tommy. Got something for you."

Tommy reacted to it being June and her habit of calling and checking on him. "Look, June, I've been working all morning on my columns. You don't need to call and make sure I'm working. I am."

"Let me start over. Not calling about your columns—but it's good to hear you're working on them. We just got a lead on a murder. We still don't have a police beat reporter, and I couldn't get hold of Vince. I think he's hiding somewhere. Anyway, this might fit into your world. The lead is, it's T.D. McFadden. He's been found shot outside his house. The cops are at the scene, not that far from you. Thought you might be interested."

"Yeah. Give me an address."

McFadden murdered? Not that long ago he was a leading citizen, before everything fell apart. Tommy's dad used to work for McFadden when he was one of the state representatives from Oklahoma County. But his insurance and car lot businesses collapsed after he was accused of crimes connected with the notorious Harris brothers and their attempt to take over a list of illicit activities left by a long-gone mobster named Big Frank Martin. McFadden was never convicted, but he lost all his customers and money. His wife divorced him after learning he had a mistress. That mistress testified against him, although she was not a believable witness, and sued him, claiming she was not his mistress at all, but a prostitute, and he hadn't paid her. The courts tossed her lawsuit because she was trying to collect a debt for illegal activity. She threatened to sue the courts, but that didn't get her anywhere either.

Suicide would be believable because McFadden's life had fallen below the gutter in a short time. He'd been one of the "normal" people who'd gone from nearly the top of the heap to rock bottom because of greed and lust, the most common among faults.

Tommy pulled onto the street, surveying the police presence. He noticed there were no TV cameras or reporters and very few neighbors gawking. It was the biggest testament to how far McFadden had fallen. He was dead and most people didn't care.

Tommy spotted a cop he knew. One who didn't hate him. "Hey, Sergeant Stevens, what's happenin'?"

"Hello, Tommy. Just your average everyday murder. There'll be an announcement soon, but looks like probably a burglary and the homeowner got shot. End of story. Gotta run."

Tommy wondered, *Do they teach cops to lie in the police academy, or is it some kind of on-the-job training?* He wouldn't learn anything by hanging around. He decided to run by the Skirvin—not exactly on his way, but he still couldn't get the Tomas matter out of his head. He had acted like it was so important to meet and then didn't show up. Something had to be wrong.

"Yes, Mister Jacks, I remember you. We called Mister Tomas's room several times this morning, and he didn't answer, so our manager opened his room. No one there. And his belongings were gone. We've contacted his office, but he's not there, either. It seems he left last night and didn't check out. The room was being billed to his paper, so maybe he figured it didn't matter. Perhaps a family emergency."

The clerk was surprisingly helpful, but his candor seemed based on a lack of suspicion that anything bad happened to Tomas. Tommy had the exact opposite reaction. Left, who knows when, and didn't check out? Made no sense. If it had been an emergency and he'd had time to pack his things, he would have stopped at the front desk and told someone something.

Tommy had to think. In a possible homage to Albright,

Tommy stopped at the downtown newsstand, purchased all that day's morning papers, and headed to Denny's on Classen. Feeling more like he was re-enacting a crime, he found an empty booth and began reading. The news was depressing. He knew as a "newspaper" person, he should do a better job of staying informed, but the more he read, the more he wanted to stop. He missed Albright. He'd been the resident grump, full of misery. It had allowed Tommy to be a cheerful adolescent—a much-preferred role.

OK Journal

My View—Tommy Jacks

Just up the page from here sits the column of George F. Barkley, the conservative editor of the *American Review* whose patrician prose has done everything possible to ensure my medicine cabinet never runs low on Pepto-Bismol.

Barkley used to play slap-and-tickle with the Freedom Branch Society until the Branchers picked on one of his favorites—former President Dwight D. Eisenhower. Out with them; they lack common sense, he sputtered. The nerve, saying Ike was a tool of the communists, etc.

But, like anybody who lives with cockroaches can tell you, driving them into dark corners and covering them up with truckloads of limestone only gives them the cover they need to multiply. The Branchers are back. Watch under your feet. It won't matter how many you stamp out. A swarm will take the place of every one you smash.

The Branchers' late founder was a former Baptist missionary who, back in the war, made Clint Eastwood look like Oliver Hardy. Evel Aloysius Branch lived by a steel-edged code, with nerve to match. He spied for the Office of Strategic Services in jungles even the Japanese wouldn't step foot in. When he came back home to Waukegan, Ill., he liked what he saw not one bit. America was circling the drain, he decided. So, he rounded up roughly two dozen other similarly war-addled veterans and hopped on a rusty freighter under sail to Bolivia, swearing by agreed oath that they'd bring Hitler back alive. That was the last anyone heard of them.

It's tough to say whether Branch, who never saw an insane risk he could resist, would hold much truck with the clutch of letter-churning conspiracy mongers the society with his name has become. But Byron Cook, the oil magnate, and the rest of the Branchers insist he's a fit symbol for their campaigns of paranoia. Besides, the dead can't sue for libel.

Barkley considers Cook and his benighted phalanx of minions as having been dealt with, even while they keep trying to sell their infection of political poison like so many cheap drug dealers.

But there's foreboding news in the hustings. The Branchers are headed this way. The festering miasma of the upcoming U.S. Senate race in Oklahoma has touched their hyper-sensitive antennae. Get ready for madness. ❧

5

SLATE ROOFS AND AGENDAS

"You actually live here?" Tommy sounded inane, gawking at his parents' new home. "I can't believe this." More college-educated insight.

Tracy and Ray stood by beaming like proud parents showing off their bundle of joy. "Pretty much over the top, isn't it? We're still kind of embarrassed, but we got a great deal." Ray still struggled with a conflict between his common-man ethics and a symbol of elitism.

"Wow. When you said you'd moved to Nichols Hills, I guess I thought it would be nice, but *wow*." Ray lived like the rich when he was young, but Tommy only knew the bottom economic rung. He'd grown up thinking, based on what he saw, that his dad didn't care for trappings of success because he was driven by more idealistic goals. Now, this. It was a shock. Of course, his dad was different after prison and especially after marrying Tracy. "Not real sure I should park my ratty old car out front," Tommy muttered.

"Well, it'll be dark soon." Ray chuckled but looked a bit embarrassed.

"Come on, Tommy. Let me show you the best part. You're not going to believe the kitchen." Tracy was just as reluctant to boast, but she was adapting faster. It was their money, and if they could afford it, which they could, she saw no reason to be anything other than happy.

"Wow."

After the "wows," they settled in to talk about work and politics, followed by a great dinner from the professional-level kitchen. Tracy smiled a lot. She said they were off the hook for Monopoly because she had an early meeting scheduled and needed her beauty sleep.

Tommy and his dad settled into a discussion with more specific details about work.

"I'm not sure about the ethics of this since technically you work for the competition," Tommy began. "I've got what I think is *potentially* a big story, but I don't know how to pursue it. You and the *Sun* would have the resources to look into it." He frowned. "But I haven't discussed this with Fred or anyone else. So, not sure I should talk about it."

Ray raised his eyebrows. "Well, that was a strange introduction. Just tell me what you're talking about, and we can decide together how to handle it. I won't run down to the paper and put out a bulletin announcing that the *Journal* has given the *Sun* a juicy lead."

Tommy grinned. Yeah, that's what they should do—not play games. Tommy related his experience with Mathew Tomas.

"He hasn't been back to work at the *Herald*. I've talked to people there about him missing our meeting, and they're concerned that something bad maybe happened. I know they've contacted the Oklahoma City police, who are handling it as a missing-person case. And it all could have nothing to do with what he wanted to talk to me about. But my gut says it did— it's because of what he wanted to talk about that he's missing."

Ray looked worried. A missing reporter with a "maybe hot" lead could be nothing, but he thought his son's instincts were correct. "I think I should approach Robbie on this, and you should talk to Bill. Maybe it's something we could handle as a joint investigation. Not sure about the details, but if we limit it to a discussion with only Robbie and Bill, and we can't agree, I won't let Robbie steal the story. If we can't agree on how to work together, we'll drop it, or I'll quit."

"I don't know, Dad. I guess I didn't realize the spot I was putting you in. Maybe we should just drop it." Tommy felt suddenly nervous. "Maybe we should just wait until the police have more time to look into this."

Ray shook his head. "I may be sitting in the middle of a very expensive house, but I'm still the same person I've always been. I can't ignore something wrong just because it might be uncomfortable. The only reason Robbie wouldn't want to pursue this would be the connection to Blackman and Connex. If he's going to take that route, I need to know now so I can get out. If Robbie's just his dad with better manners, I will not work for him. Period."

Tommy shook his head, already regretting bringing it up. Tracy would kill him if his dad got fired or quit. "Look, Dad— just give it a week. I think there's too much risk right now for us to try and make anything happen. We don't know how Robbie will react or how Bill will react. Suppose Bill says he can't believe I shared privileged information with the *Sun* and decides to fire me. How would you feel?"

It didn't sound like Bill Anderson, but he had become a different person since Ray first knew him. Who knew what he might do? "Okay. We'll give it a week."

Tommy considered telling Ray he thought he saw Chuck Branson at the Skirvin on the same day Tomas disappeared but decided he'd blabbed enough for one day. They chatted about less ominous subjects until Tommy went home.

His small, messy apartment made him smile; he was comfortable where he was. He was sure that would change, probably under Patsy's influence. Still, he cared little about money. He did, however, know his thoughts about success had changed. He wanted to wield some influence, and the only way to do that was to achieve success. He'd actually planned to talk to Tracy that night about appearing on her show, but he didn't. He rationalized he still needed to decide how to approach the subject.

Also among his secret feelings was the envy he felt when he heard Albright announce he was going to publish a book.

He wasn't the pure-hearted kid he used to be. He had ambitions.

The slates for the U.S. Senate primaries began to take shape. Some candidates hadn't filed all the paperwork yet, but the gossipmongers were already handicapping the field. Anyone with knowledge of the inner workings of Oklahoma politics was already giving the best odds to Blackman on the Republican ticket and Fillmore on the Democratic side. Blackman was an overwhelming overall favorite, with most people giving no chance to anyone else. This was largely based on the assumption he'd get the endorsement of the *Sun*, the current Governor Evans, and the departing Senator Butler. No other candidate could match that trifecta.

On the Democratic side, most believed it a possibility, if slight, that Fillmore might lose to either of his anticipated primary opponents, Bruce Irving and Nick Hightower. Most in-the-know folks thought Fillmore was too liberal to be elected in Oklahoma. It had been a strong Democratic state for many years but was quickly becoming a Republican stronghold, and Fillmore was considered as being to the left of most Democrats who remained. He was a liberal college president in a state not known for electing people based on intelligence. The only reason some touts picked Fillmore was the long odds. It was part of the game.

In his favor were public speaking skills and populist ideas. There was still a bubbling populist movement in Oklahoma looking for a champion, and he fit the bill. He would be attacked as a communist, even if everyone knew that was not true, and labeled as anti-Christian based on some imaginary link in many people's minds between communism and non-believers. Most Oklahomans hardly knew what communism was and only concluded it to be un-American. The word itself generated fear and loathing among most of them, even if they might admit their own class struggle against powerful elites who controlled their lives. But at least they sure as hell weren't communists. They were Republicans.

Irving and Hightower described themselves as farmers and ranchers, although it wasn't clear whether either owned a farm or a ranch. Both worked in government, sort of.

Irving was one of two employees in the Peanut Commission, part of the Oklahoma Department of Agriculture. His exact job was unclear. When asked by a reporter to describe what he did, he said, "No comment." Apparently, the paper noted wryly, his job was top secret.

Hightower's connection to farms and ranches was yet murkier. He was listed as a part-time deputy sheriff for the Osage County Sheriff's Department. When contacted by the *Tulsa Herald,* the department's spokesperson said she wasn't sure about the last time he'd worked there, but she'd check and get back to them. She didn't. He had also run as an independent candidate for mayor of Pawhuska some years back and received eighty-five votes.

One observer noted that a lack of more qualified candidates on the Democratic side meant the Republican, meaning Blackman, should win. Rich, powerful, oil company tycoon—how could he lose?

The two other candidates on the Republican side were party loyalists who'd held office before. From Oklahoma City came ex-councilman Frank Clayton, and from Tulsa, County Commissioner Sam Elliot. In private, both supported Blackman, so maybe they ran only to give an appearance of a contested race. Still, they raised impressive contributions considering the long odds.

Outside the two-party umbrella ran an independent candidate, Oliver Howser, and a candidate for the United Workers of America Party named Mike Smith. Insiders said Howser was most likely crazy and would provide some interesting moments, but otherwise he would be a non-factor. Smith was so serious he'd never been seen smiling. He seemed to advocate something closer to citizen revolt than merely electing him as senator. He was indeed a communist. But in an odd twist of life, common to the prairie, he also was a lay minister for a nameless church in Pawnee.

Beyond the primaries, the know-it-alls predicted Henry Blackman to win in a Republican landslide because the state's voters now strongly leaned Republican and because of the money and connections his campaign already had. It didn't matter who the Democratic candidate turned out to be.

One pundit noted in a *Tulsa Herald* opinion piece, "it should be entertaining, if nothing else."

OK Journal

My View—Tommy Jacks

The primary election for the U.S. Senate seat that Republican Rick Butler's so anxious to bail out of is only a bit more than a year away. What better way to make that time pass like torturous eternity than to stuff the ranks with the most Sheol-worthy candidates this side of the Styx?

Let's not forget the impish semi-legion of the Freedom Branch Society about to come riding their mangy were-coyotes down from Kansas, bent to make sure everything is bloody and paranoiac.

Their first target, says my source who practices law among just the sorts who keep their noses low enough to the ground for matters like that, is Howard Fillmore, president of Corinthian Oklahoma College and probably the only candidate who can spell "Senate." He's a Democrat, first of all, and everyone knows what's been happening lately for them. But Republicans don't take, let alone give, chances. So far, the only other Democrats who seem interested are some guy who, according to the same source, is a deep clandestine operative for the state Peanut Commission, and another guy who just might be out patrolling the tallgrass prairie in Osage County as a deputy sheriff. Or maybe not.

Then there's an independent candidate, Oliver Howser, about whom it's been tough to get a line on. The source just shrugs. "Ne-e-ever heard of him."

But he'd heard of Mike Smith, the United Workers of America's Party's best and brightest, who doesn't mind admitting he's a real, honest-to-gosh communist.

Word is, the Branch Bunch doesn't like him, but they won't sniff at such a small potato. They're licking their chops for Fillmore, already basting him as "anti-Christian" and "pro-communist," and whatever other multi-syllabic epithets they can mispronounce.

Their strategy, by the way, seems to be to clear the field for Henry Blackman, the blackguard king of Connex, one of the oil giants settled like a putrescent beached whale on the state's landscape. Connex has yet to offer to repay the tax breaks that led it to slump into Oklahoma like a Komodo dragon chomping its way along a chum line of fish heads.

Frank Clayton, who once served two terms on the Oklahoma City Council, and Sam Elliott, who has made his fortune as a Tulsa County commissioner, *say* they're in the primary against Blackman. But the smart money tells a different story: that they'll disappear before next August if it starts to look like Fillmore doesn't have the strength to send the Branchers yelping away.

Indeed, reading the list and running down the facts leads straight into the downward spiral that Dante said began with the words over the gate, *Lasciate ogni speranza, voi ch'intrate*— "Abandon all hope, you who enter." If you read "Inferno," you'll remember every hopeless inmate of hell had a speech to give, fit to print, verbatim.

Beware. That's how they keep you moving along the trip downward with them: the speeches. ❧

6

TURN LEFT AHEAD

The campus of Corinthian Oklahoma College stood in the middle of a wheat field south of Enid with five buildings and two dormitories. It was founded in 1928 by Lester Holmes, a rustic Renaissance man of oil and cattle, as a gift to his wife. She'd always wanted to teach at a college, and she did for three years before conceding that young people were too annoying. Lester only shrugged. His initial investment and future endowment didn't take much out of his pocket, so he never regretted it.

The school's history was full of instances when it appeared it would have to close due to poor enrollment or finances. But somehow, often because of efforts of current and past students, it managed to survive. Most of its alumni were not famous or rich, but almost all described their experiences at COC as the best times of their lives. The school did not major in marketable skills, but offered a respectful environment wherein young people could learn to grow beyond the limits of being students in the middle of a wheat field south of Enid, Oklahoma. Its alumni were well represented in the sciences and arts. Few were politicians.

"Welcome, Tommy. It's good to see you again," Howard Fillmore offered a warm greeting.

"I've never been here before. It's a great campus. How many students do you have?" Tommy thought the college looked more like an eastern school than one from western Oklahoma.

"About eighteen hundred, and that's pushing our limit. Most have a parent who attended, maybe a grandparent. It helps to have a long history."

"How did you end up here?"

"My sister came here. I was working at Oklahoma State in Stillwater, and I'd visit her. I fell in love with Corinthian— really, the idea of the place. Today it seems all the emphasis in higher education is to prepare students for some kind of employment. But the emphasis here has always been and still is to prepare them for life. It seemed like a sanctuary to me. When they had the opening, I lobbied really hard for the job." Fillmore smiled.

At a small, round table Tommy got out his pad and pen. "So, why would you want to be a U.S. Senator and move away from this?"

Fillmore laughed. "I'm not sure I do." He continued more seriously. "I believe in this country. I know there are many people who have questioned my patriotism, but it's because of my love of country that I feel I must speak out. I think we're headed in the wrong direction, and I can't just sit back and not do something."

"Are you a communist?"

He chuckled. "No. Despite the rumors, I'm not." He paused. "I do think the government has a role to play in our lives. I might even suggest that role is vital in making us a better country and creating a fairer system. But I don't believe the government should own and run everything. If someone wants to call me a communist because they can't defend their own beliefs, then it's their problem, and not mine."

Tommy smiled. "Off the record—you really think you can win?"

"Sure. And that can be on the record. Of course, I need to win the primary first. I've heard there are two other candidates announced so far. I'll state my case as to why citizens should vote for me, and I intend to win. If I do, you can come back and ask me if I think I can win the general election. I think my answer would once again be, 'Yes.' "

They went on to discuss some specific issues regarding federal regulations and agriculture issues impacting the state. Fillmore was candid and provided detailed, thoughtful responses.

"Do you think the U.S. should get out of Vietnam?"

"We should never get involved in a war without a complete understanding of what we're doing and how we win or end it. Vietnam has been a mistake from the beginning. Just because we made a mistake years ago and got into this mess is no reason to stay. The Nixon administration has mishandled every aspect of this conflict and has lied to Americans. Given the opportunity, I would vote as a senator to leave Vietnam at once. You may not know this, but the Vietnamese call the war 'the resistance against America,' or 'the American War.' We're the invaders. I think we need to rethink the whole idea that we have a right to tell other people how to live in their own country."

"The latest Associated Press poll shows that a slight majority of Oklahomans support the war. Can you run on an antiwar platform and win?"

"I believe many people support the war because they want

to support their country. But the leaders have misled them and should be held accountable. Staying in a bad war because we don't have the guts to end it is not a good solution. I think I can talk to Oklahomans about that, and while we may disagree, I don't believe they'd vote against me just on this one issue. I think most people will agree something has to change."

Tommy wrapped up. "Thank you, Doctor Fillmore. I appreciate your candid responses."

"Well, thank you, Tommy. And by the way, just call me Howard. That 'Doctor' title is a little too stuffy for me."

Tommy smiled. "I want to wish you the best. You'd make a great senator for this state, and the nation." They shook hands.

"Be sure and add your endorsement to your column." Fillmore patted Tommy on the back while he walked him out.

Tommy thought a lot about Fillmore on the drive back to the capitol. He was a good man living in a state that didn't see the world like he did. Blackman would be the Republican candidate, and Fillmore had almost no chance of defeating him. Tommy knew he should remain impartial. But he couldn't help feeling angry that the best man wouldn't win.

In the press room he found a note from Tracy. She'd dropped by to see him and wanted to talk. She'd be home the rest of the day. That was unusual. He called first, but she didn't answer. She hadn't noted the time on her message, so maybe she wasn't home yet. He headed out to the new house.

He rang the doorbell. Tracy, still dressed for work, answered. "Everything okay?" he asked. "I got your note."

"I should've left you a hint—it's nothing bad, okay?" She

gave him a hug. Ever since Tracy came into his dad's and his life, everybody hugged.

"Patsy says I'm worse than a mother hen." He still looked worried.

Tracy laughed. "You need to marry her before she gets away. Hear me?"

"I've asked her, but she says I'm still a baby."

They went into the kitchen where Tracy made iced tea. "My boss—speaking of babies—was talking about you. He knows I married your dad, but since I kept my maiden name for the show, I think he hasn't realized we're related. People like him aren't geniuses. Anyway, he wants to know if you'll do a weekly interview segment. Your column's a huge hit, and people talk about it every time a new one comes out. So, Mister Genius thinks it would make great TV for you to interview politicians. He was dropping ideas like 'Jacks's Corner,' or 'Jacks's Time.'"

That caught him off guard. "TV? Um, I have real mixed feelings. I'll admit I've thought about it—even almost asked you. But I'm not so sure. I'm afraid of screwing up. What do you think?"

"I hadn't imagined it either. But the more I thought about it, the better the idea got. I think you'd be great. And a more news-oriented segment would be a huge improvement over Betty's latest gardening tips."

He narrowed his eyes for comic effect. "I watch Betty. And I don't even have a garden."

She slumped. "I know. Half our fan mail goes to her. It's just that she's dumb as dirt." She looked at Tommy and they shared a long laugh.

"But really," he asked at last, "you think I should do it?"

"I think the paper will want you to, I think it'll be good for your career, and I think TV is where more people get their news and information. You need to get involved."

"Yeah. Troubles me, though. I just interviewed Fillmore, and I wore my old blue jeans, we chatted back and forth, some on the record, some off. I just don't know about doing an interview with people there to watch. Not saying I won't. But it'll be different. And I'm not sure in a good way. I think it will lose something."

She nodded. "It will. People trust you when you talk to them one-on-one. The camera makes it a show, and you lose the trust. But," she smiled, "it'd be great to have you on my show. That would make me real proud."

Making your mom proud was the best reason so far. He knew once Bill and Fred heard, they would insist. So he figured he might as well do it, and not fight city hall. "Have any idea who would be the first interview?"

"The boy genius said he already has a commitment from Henry Blackman." Tracy smiled.

Wasn't that just great!

OK Journal

My View—Tommy Jacks

You can't get more Oklahoma than Enid. The plains there stretch all the way to the tip of the Texas stovepipe, south to the Red River and north to Nebraska. The view of approaching tornados must be spectacular on a sweltering summer afternoon.

If you set down a building of any size there, it has to stick out. There's hardly anything else to interrupt the ocean of grass aside from Vance Air Force Base.

A bit south of town the administration building, stately classroom warrens and dormitories of Corinthian Oklahoma College stand like a collection of abandoned, ornate boxes. There's ivy, too, like you'd expect at a place dedicated to contemplation and learning in the so-called liberal arts.

Howard Fillmore, president of the college, would explain that "liberal arts" only means a range of subjects that tend to connect, like philosophy, language, arts and the like, more than, say, the practical sciences. But that "liberal" part will cling to him like ivy every step of the campaign trail while he seeks the nomination of the Democratic Party for the upcoming U.S. Senate race.

"Liberal" is a venomous word

on the plains, even if used for technically correct reasons. Whether you understand what it or its opposite number, "conservative," means isn't the point. The point is that here in the middle of America, anybody who doesn't keep in step with a political culture that values bombs and petroleum more than education and openness is labeled "liberal," and forcibly lashed to worse adjectives, like "un-American."

That's what we've learned in three short years of covering politics in this state where much of the ground lays flat, and people like Fillmore and places like his college stand out. It doesn't matter whether saying, "Staying in a bad war because we don't have the guts to end it is not a good solution" might have more to do with patriotism—another word so misused we've lost its meaning—than politics.

What matters is how certain people are going to use certain words over the next year and three or so months, and whether they can get everyone else to react to them the way they do. Could anything more cynical, anti-human and essentially unpatriotic be imaginable? ❦

7
COMINGS AND GOINGS

"Press room. Tommy Jacks."

"Jacks, I'm Dick Fitzgerald; do the police beat for the *Tulsa Herald*. And I'm a friend of Matt Tomas. Got a minute?"

Tommy sat up. "What can I do for you?"

Fitzgerald sighed. "I'm pretty sure Matt's dead. There's no way he'd just disappear. I talked to him around three or so the day he went missing. Told me he was going to give you what he knew about Blackman. I think that asshole had him killed. Matt had been workin' on this for months, and while he couldn't prove it, he figured Blackman was rigging the inventory numbers to make it look like those tank farms were full. And I can tell you that's true because I've climbed on most of those damned tanks. They're empty."

"I'm worried, too. I only met him that day, but he seemed like a nice guy. Did Blackman know he was investigating him?"

"Oh, sure. He's got a pet thug named Ed Black. Ed confronted Matt a couple of weeks ago. Told him he'd better keep clear of their tanks or they'd have him arrested. That was here in the newsroom, at the paper—just walked in here and threatened him. But there was no way he would stop."

Tommy felt powerless but asked anyway. "How can I help?"

"I'm not sure. Not even sure why I called. But it just seems nothing's being done. I talked to your police chief, guy named Lawson. He was concerned, but he said they didn't have any leads and they're more or less stumped. It's just frustrating. I know something bad's happened, and I can't do anything."

"I know Lawson. I'll go talk to him. Tomas disappeared while he was in town, and the police can't just shrug it off. I'll make some noise in my column. Don't know if that'll get any action, but at least it's something."

"Guess I still owe you that interview I promised. It's been so busy around here. Maybe next month some time—would that work?" Chief Lawson was quiet, polite, and business-like, the exact opposite of Underwood, who was all bluster and no substance. After Underwood was gunned down, Lawson faced the task of cleaning up a department that had sunk closer to a gang of rogues than cops.

Tommy's experience with the police had mostly been a disaster until Lawson took over. "Sure, chief. Just let me know."

"But what can I do for you today?"

"A couple of things. The first has to do with the disappearance of Mathew Tomas, the reporter for the *Tulsa Herald*. He came to that symposium at the Skirvin, and he's missing. Do you have anything on that?"

Lawson grimaced. "This whole thing's just terrible. A guest in our city goes missing, and we have no idea how or why. We first thought he'd left for personal reasons and he'd pop back up in a day or two. It's frustrating, but we don't have anything to go on."

"The hotel staff said all his belongings were gone. Nobody

saw when he left?"

"We questioned every staff person at the hotel. We questioned every guest on his floor. We've canvassed the neighborhood with pictures of him. We talked to both cab companies working that part of town. We've come up empty."

Tommy was not surprised the new chief had the department operating in a more professional manner, but it didn't help his sense that something was overlooked. "What can you do now?"

"You're going to hate this, but all we can do is wait. Something has to happen to give us a lead. This sort of thing isn't as uncommon as you might think. Adult males disappear all the time. Bad marriage, hate their kids, work sucks, something makes them want a new life, and they just walk. They're missing persons because they want to be. I'm not saying that about Tomas. I'm just saying we don't know what happened, and until we get a lead, we're stumped."

"One thing I know is that he was working on what could be a big story about a prominent person here. I don't believe he'd walk away from that." Tommy felt sure some harm had come to Tomas.

Lawson sat up a little. "What 'prominent person'?"

Tommy hesitated, regretting that he mentioned it. "This is tricky. You know we don't talk about stuff we can't print. Tomas had worked on this for months, but never had enough facts to write anything. If I tell you who, and you pursue that person as a possible suspect in Tomas's disappearance based on my word, I'd be at risk professionally."

The chief nodded. "I'll protect you as a source, guaranteed. But if you know something that will help us find him, you need to share that. I can't force you. But," he raised his eyebrows, "withholding information can be a crime."

"Is that a threat, chief?"

"No. Let me back up. I know your experience with this department has been a nightmare. The old chief was a crook, and he ran it like a personal gang. But most of us here are good people trying to make things better. And you and I have gotten to known each other a little. I hope you feel like you can trust me."

Tommy still wasn't sure, but said, "Henry Blackman."

"The oil guy who's running for Senate?"

"Yeah. Tomas believed he was committing fraud by faking inventory in his oil tanks. He's using that as collateral in his stock offering. We're talking millions. One of my sources says Blackman's security guy threatened Tomas just a few days ago." Tommy did not like this turn of events but couldn't just withhold what he knew. He added how he knew all that but figured his perhaps imaginary sighting of Chuck Branson was too weird to pass along.

"I appreciate you trusting me. I'll see if we can't get some photos of Blackman and his security guy and show them around. Might get somethin'. What's the security guy's name?"

Tommy couldn't recall. "Not sure."

"We'll find out."

"The other thing's the murder of T.D. McFadden. Any leads?"

"Sounds like you're tracking our failures." The chief looked serious.

"No, it's not that. Just that I was out at his house the day he was discovered, and it seemed like no one cared. Anything happening?"

"Once again," Lawson sighed, "we don't have much. He was shot with a small-caliber gun, which we didn't find. Shot only once in the head. We heard maybe he was involved in some of that drug stuff with the Harris brothers, but we don't have any evidence, and Dealin' Dave says T.D. didn't have anything to do with it. Ex-wife's in Florida, and she didn't seem real interested one way or the other, also she has an ironclad alibi. His very ex-girlfriend hates him, but she's not a suspect. Nothing was taken from the house that we can tell, so probably not a burglary gone bad. At this point, it's a lot like the Tomas matter. We're just waiting to see if we get some more information." He shrugged. "Somethin' will break. At least we hope. It's not anything we want put in the papers—but sometimes the bad guys win." He looked like he'd aged years in the few months he had been the police chief.

Tommy called his father from the press room. "Hey, Dad. Been thinking about when we talked about Matt Tomas and trying to get our bosses to form a team. I want to do that."

"Me, too. You need to talk to Bill, and I'll go see Robbie right now. Did something happen?"

"No. It's because nothing is happening."

"Press room. Jacks."

"Glad to see you're becoming more abrupt and surly. You must be livin' the good life in God's country," Taylor Albright replied.

"Hey, Taylor. Figured once you got back to the civilized world, we'd never hear from you again."

"Kinda surprises me, too. I've persuaded my newsstand guy to carry the *OK Journal,* so I read your stuff. Not exactly *Banner* level, yet, but you're getting there." Albright chuckled. "What do you think is going to happen in the Senate race?"

Why would a New York City resident care about that? Tommy answered, "My pick would be Blackman, likely by a landslide. But that's not what *should* happen. Fillmore's about the smartest person I've met, apart from you. And he's a lot nicer. So, he'd be a great senator. But no way in hell will he win."

"I talked to your dad this morning. He said there might be some pretty ugly skeletons in Blackman's closet. Do you think that could trip him up?"

Tommy settled his elbows on the desk. "Okay, Mister Albright, what's really going on? You didn't call just to chat. And why all this interest in the Senate race?"

"You're just as annoying over the phone as you are in person. How could Fillmore win?"

"The odds are long. Louongo says the Freedom Branch Society will go after him, hard. The state guy for the Branchers is gonna make all kinds of noise about Fillmore being a communist. And Fillmore himself won't help matters because he's running on an anti-war position. So, all that says if he has a chance, it's based on two things. One is that something might come out about Blackman. I think there are some strange things involving him and his company. The other's if people actually listen to what Fillmore's saying. I know it's a cliché, but this guy really cares. If they can screen out the nonsense, who knows? He might win."

"Bill Anderson asked me to be Fillmore's campaign manager. What do you think?"

Tommy was stunned. Albright had been Anderson's campaign manager many years ago when he ran for governor. They suffered a narrow but devastating loss. "Are you a masochist? Why would you want to come back to Oklahoma to run a losing campaign? Haven't you had enough of that?"

"Good question. Not sure I know the answer. I do know that Fillmore is the kind of person who should be leading this country, not Blackman. And how can I ignore that and just pretend it'll all work out? If I can help, I have no choice but to try."

The right answer. But Albright could only compound Fillmore's misfit-outsider problems. What was Anderson thinking?

OK Journal

My View—Tommy Jacks

Painful as it is to remember, let alone admit, I've been closer to the heat of real, live, lead-bullet battle than I'd prefer. And my travels have never taken me closer to Hue or Pleiku than the loop I took with my uncle from Los Angeles through the great Northwest, one summer back when I was in junior high, which is another story for another time.

All that's only to confirm it's true what they say about the chaotic maelstrom of war that trashes all the rules of conduct, physics, life and, I'm afraid, death, all at once and on the fly. You don't think, you react. Your first thought is, "Don't get killed," and your second is, "Don't hurt anyone." Heroes get killed. Cowards strike, flee and survive. The cheaters, the lowest of the low, keep coming back. And the devilish business keeps going, full blast.

Now we're about to walk head-on into another firefight, about fourteen months long. Once it gets going, toss your political compass. It's nigh impossible to keep track of the players, or to tell why they're even in it, whether it's for all the right reasons, or for the money, or just because they're irretrievably hooked on the rush they get from what amounts to booby-trapping entire populations.

For some, each victory, pyrrhic and blood-soaked as it might be, is a step closer to the resurrection of the idea of concentration camps to preserve and promote their ideals of dominance. And that all sounds and smells hyperbolic, but it's just what politicians do to keep your attention. But you don't have to humor them, or us. You should, however, take a long, critical, serious look.

The armies of the north are on the march. A detachment of the Freedom Branch Society has mobilized, presumably in support of whoever will be the Republican nominee for the Senate seat to be exited two Januaries from now by good old Rick Butler. The serious monies on Henry Blackman, the oil baron so rough-edged, he even smells like a used 55-gallon drum.

On the other side is Howard Fillmore, president of Corinthian Oklahoma College, and the very man who took a regiment of journalists to task a couple of weeks ago, telling us just how much grip we'd lost on the realities of our job. He's getting help, but we fear it's the kind that will only dig his ideological hole deeper, as far as the yokels in charge of political labels in this state are concerned.

Just seeing all that coming tells us the bullets will likely start flying thick, fast and sooner than any of us can be comfortable with. Forget campaign buttons. Get helmets and flak vests. And stay indoors. This is going to get nasty. 🐝

8
A STAR IS BORN

Part of Tommy wanted to try TV, and the rest was terrified. His ambition pushed for a bigger audience. The more reserved part pleaded for the shadows.

The show's producer had Tommy do practice sessions in which he was coached on how to act, look, talk, smile, breathe. The guy was the most annoying person Tommy'd ever met. In the newspaper business, he'd probably be killed and stuffed into a closet. But in TV world, he was a star. It was all based on ratings—high ratings, you're a hero; low, you're gone.

Today would be his interview with Henry Blackman, live. Tommy suggested it might be better to start with a couple of lesser personalities, but the boy genius said that would only ruin the suspense. "People will watch just to see if you screw up."

Not exactly what Tommy needed to hear.

"You look a little pale," observed Tracy, the one person on the set who actually cared how well he might do.

"I don't think more makeup will help. I think I might faint." He felt intimidated by the crowd gathered in the station to bear witness.

She turned him by the shoulders to look at her. "Look. You've got to put all of them out of your mind. And just forget you're on TV. How many people have you interviewed? Hundreds? Just do it like it's you and Blackman. Ask the questions *you* would ask, not what the creep producer wants. Do it your way, or not at all." She was in his face. She had his attention. "Think about it, Tommy. What's the worst that can happen? You get fired? Do you really give a shit if you are? No. You're a newspaper columnist. If this goes bad, you can write about it for weeks. It'll be gold for your column—you can make fun of TV people. Ask the hard questions. You're good at this. Now, go show them how a real journalist does it."

He just stared for a moment. Then he hugged her. "Thanks."

"Welcome to *Oklahoma AM,* Mister Blackman." Tommy managed not to flub that. So far, so good.

"Thanks, Tommy. I read your column all the time. It's great, even though I have a feeling we may not be on the same political team."

"Columnists have opinions about everything. That's part of the job." Tommy smiled but did not feel friendly. "Tell us, why do you want to be a U.S. Senator?"

"Might as well get right to the point, huh? First, I am a strong believer in this country being the greatest that the world has ever seen. I think we're blessed by God to have such a wonderful place to call home. The God-given freedoms we have in this country are unique to America, and every one of us must be ready to fight to keep those freedoms for our future generations. I've been fortunate to experience the huge opportunity that exists here, like no other place on this planet, to succeed. I'm just an ordinary person who's been fortunate to live in this great country and the great state of Oklahoma, and I've achieved success beyond my wildest dreams. Now I think it's time I paid back some of that great fortune by serving my country so everyone can have the opportunities I've had."

It was live TV, so Tommy was acutely aware it would be a mistake to laugh out loud, tempting as it was. He had trouble thinking of the next question beyond, *are you kidding me?*

"I would imagine your opponents believe in this country as much as you. What makes you better qualified?"

"Well some of 'em do, and some of 'em don't." There seemed an edge to Blackman's tone. "I know my primary opponents are all God-fearing Americans. Not so sure about some of those Democrats." Blackman smiled but it seemed more of a sneer.

"Are you saying Democrats aren't Americans?"

"Maybe. I've heard lots of strange things about that guy Fillmore, who I guess is their frontrunner. Not saying he's not American, just saying he believes a lot of bullshit I don't believe, lots of communist crap that just does not belong in this country." There were audible gasps behind the bright lights. One couldn't say "bullshit" on TV without risk of losing a license. Various station people signaled Tommy to go to a commercial break.

"Looks like we're going to a commercial. We'll be right back with the Republican candidate for U.S. Senate, Mister Henry Blackman."

"Okay, you're off."

The boy genius was on the stage, sweating. "Shit, man! You can't say 'bullshit' on live TV." His dreams were collapsing before his eyes.

"Don't tell me what to say, you little piece of shit. If something's bullshit, I'll say it's bullshit." Blackman stood and ripped off his microphone. "I don't know about you, Jacks. Maybe you're not my kind of guy." He stormed off, followed by his small entourage.

"Guess that didn't go so well," Tommy mumbled. Now what?

Now the show's producer was the one who looked pale. "We'll be back on the air in ten seconds. Just say Blackman wasn't able to stay due to a previous commitment, and hand it back to Tracy, okay?"

The director signaled Tommy that he was back on the air. "I'm sure if you were watching before, you saw and heard Mister Blackman say a 'no-no' on TV. Hope nobody was too offended. I'm sure we've all heard worse. And we don't really know if Mister Blackman regrets what he said, because he decided to leave. This is my first live TV interview, and I must say it was interesting. As Mister Blackman said during the interview, he and I may not share political beliefs about a lot of things, but something I think we can agree on is that honest opinions from our leaders always have value. So, I fully support Mister Blackman's right to state his opinion, even if his choice of words might've been better. I hope we'll have more interviews with our political leaders. Not only are they informative and can make us better citizens, they're also occasionally entertaining. Thanks for watching. Back to you, Tracy." Tommy was already feeling great relief, expecting he would be fired. He was already making plans for a nap.

"Shit, shit, shit! I told you to give it back to Tracy, not conduct a damn monologue. Is everybody nuts today?" The producer headed off, shaking his head and waving his arms.

Tracy came up to give Tommy a hug. "Welcome to live TV."

The drama and trauma compelled Tommy to stop at Del Rancho on his way to the *OK Journal* headquarters. He needed something to help settle his nerves before he talked with Bill Anderson. When life gives you lemons, chow down on a chicken-fried steak sandwich, fries, and a Coke, and all will be better. The need for a nap became pressing. He hoped Anderson perhaps hadn't watched.

"Saw you on TV this morning. That was a very impressive debut." Bill smiled.

Tommy wasn't sure whether "impressive" meant good or bad. "Didn't exactly go as planned. Blackman seems a little volatile."

"More like crazy. I've never heard a more pompous speech. I thought you did a great job. It's a shame he left—I was looking forward to the rest. Of course, I'm supporting Fillmore, so maybe I'm a little biased."

He seemed in a good mood, so Tommy decided to get it over with. "Mister Anderson, I've been working on something and getting nowhere. I have an idea you may not like. But I think if you will give it some thought, you'll see it's worth pursuing even if it is a little unusual."

Bill looked interested, if a little apprehensive. Tommy gave him the background on Mathew Tomas, his disappearance, and suspicions that Blackman could be involved in something illegal. From there he jumped into his discussion and conclusions between him and his dad. He thought if Bill was going to get mad, it would be at that point, but he didn't.

"I would've never thought we could cooperate on something like what you're suggesting. But maybe since your dad's there, we could. I know they have better investigative resources than we do. And we both have an interest in protecting journalists. What would trouble me is that I expect the *Sun* to endorse Blackman, and we're going to endorse Fillmore, if they win their primaries. That's a lot to overlook. Do you think it could work?"

"Not sure, Mister Anderson. I don't know Mister Gilmore, but my dad seems to think he can overlook the impact on Blackman and just go after the truth. Not sure if he's discussed it with Mister Gilmore yet. I think that's the real question: will the *Sun* investigate someone they plan to endorse?"

"If Robbie would say yes, I would, too. If he says no, we'll pursue it the best we can. And if Robbie tries to use this information to hurt us or Fillmore, it'll be on him—not you or your father. But I think Robbie might do it. The good side is that if he can prove Blackman isn't doing all that, it'll make him feel better about his endorsement. Sort of along the lines of your speech today."

Robbie Gilmore frowned thoughtfully. "Ray, you're asking me to join with the *Journal* to investigate the man I want to be our next U.S. Senator?"

"I guess the answer is, 'Yes.'" Ray felt like a big "no" was headed his way, leaving him in the position of having to resign. He didn't feel well.

Robbie looked thoughtful. "You know," he replied, "I've had my own doubts about Blackman. Look at what he did this morning with your son. The guy's a buffoon. But I don't think he's a crook. Still, I like this idea a lot—a combined task force to investigate events directly impacting the state or even the nation. That'd bring a lot of firepower to bear on some key issues. I can even see how it could help both papers. Our stories about the investigations would be slightly different from theirs. It's so intriguing. Plus, you may not believe this, but the one person I absolutely trust in this world is Bill Anderson. Isn't that ironic?"

"There's something I need to confess. I told Tommy that if you didn't do this, there would be only one reason—your endorsement of Blackman. And if that happened, I couldn't work for you. Just listening to you, I realized I was wrong. There's a lot to consider, and it's your right to endorse a buffoon. And I have no right to dictate my employment based on you agreeing with my politics. So, whatever you decide on this joint investigation will be fine with me."

Robbie nodded. "I'll contact Bill and we'll get this started. I'll endorse a buffoon, but not a crook. Get to work and find out if he deserves my endorsement—or not."

OK Journal

My View—Tommy Jacks

No sense trying to duck. It looks, feels and smells official. Yours most truly has joined, albeit with grave reluctance, the clutch of nattering nabobs of negativism on the tube.

A segment of "Oklahoma AM" dedicated to early risers and pitiable insomniacs, and which I've been given to handle, has a name I haven't quite caught on to, yet. I have a suggestion based on what it's been so far: "Unmitigated Disasters, Featuring the Ink-Stained Wretch." To make things even better, its producer has a track record of dismissing helpful suggestions with an angry sneer and language we're not allowed to use in a newspaper.

Speaking of language, we've just discovered that early-morning television is the place to go if you crave to expand your vocabulary creatively. Henry Blackman, the oil tycoon sort who came on as my first interview subject, took the floor as our instructor and delivered a lesson with blinding speed. I can't say what might have been asked or uttered by myself or the producer that started it. I'm not used to such early hours yet, and coffee only makes my brain cells do doughnut spins against the roof of my skull. But the next thing I know, the man's bellowing an FCC-forbidden two-syllable oath like a charging bull elk.

Come to think of it, I believe "bull" was part of what he said.

Whatever, it had the effect of a magic spell. The producer hyperventilated. His eyeballs turned upward in their sockets. Cooler heads among the squadron of technicians—at least, the ones who hadn't withered to the floor in dead faints—flashed frenzied semaphore signals toward a crack team hidden behind suspiciously dark panes of glass. Just like that, we were off the air, replaced by an uninterrupted parade of commercials for Frisbees, Red Goose shoes and Buicks.

I just sat, gaping like Bobo the Simpleminded, watching the producer and Blackman go at it like Rod Laver and Ken Rosewall, using the same expletive for a ball. Blackman ripped off his lapel mike—I believe with his teeth, although I could have hallucinated under duress of hysteria—and stalked out, leaving steaming shoeprints in the treated-concrete studio floor.

To be frank, the word Blackman used is one that fairly 95 percent of us not only hear, but also use just about every day, in circumstances that spread from the mindlessly casual to the flagrantly urgent. No surveys were done, but it seems fair to assume a good chunk of the audience hardly noticed it. However, one of the call-ins after the show remarked that he or she wished everybody could be as honest and true to themselves as Blackman seemed.

"Doesn't mean I want to vote for him," the caller's note read, "but I give him points for being unpretentious."

Almost everyone else, especially the producer, wanted to forget it. I hoped that meant they wanted to forget me, too, but no such luck. See you next time. And believe me, I'll watch my language. ❧

9
FIRE DANCE

"Welcome to the first meeting of the Joint Investigative Group, or 'JIG.' So we can continue, let's all say something like, 'the jig is up,' and get it out of our systems." Nobody did, but everyone snickered. "My name's Ray Jacks. You all know me one way or another. The first thing we're going to do is be candid about what's happening here: *We don't know*. Yep, that's it—we don't know what's happening. We're here to find out. Since there's never been a JIG before, we'll all learn what works best and what doesn't. Any questions?"

Vince Young had one. "Aren't you the famous Tommy Jacks's dad?"

"Very funny, Vince. That's the next rule: no humor in this group. Got it?" Ray mock-frowned. "Just kidding. And yes, I am the famous TV star Tommy Jacks's dad. Matter of fact, would you like to say a few words, Tommy, before we move forward?"

"Only that I'm not responsible for Vince Young."

"So," Ray took back up, "let me introduce everyone. From the *Sun*, we have Mike Sanders and Janet Davis. From the *Journal*, Vince Young and Tommy Jacks. And on special assignment from the *Tulsa Herald*, Dick Fitzgerald. I think most of you know one another, and if not, you will quickly. There'll be others who'll join us, although I think this is a pretty formidable group." Ray beamed like a proud coach of the winning team. "Now to the serious part. How do we find out what happened to our colleague Mathew Tomas?"

They went over everything known, their insights and their questions. Ray handed out assignments and discussed their next meeting which was in about a week. They understood it was extra work for everyone. Each had a regular job to handle besides JIG work.

"What do you think?" Ray quizzed Tommy in the hall later.

Tommy shrugged. "Let's see what it looks like in a few days. We need some kind of break to give us direction. A real key is going to be Fitzgerald and his research on the Connex's financial records. As far as finding Tomas," he sighed, "I think we're too late."

Ray nodded. "Yeah."

"Also, I think we should hire Louongo."

"I'm way ahead of you. Got budget authorization this morning. He'll be on board starting tomorrow."

When looking for evil, you need someone who knows where evil lives: Joe Louongo, Esquire.

Henry Blackman was not a happy man. There was that fiasco of an interview in Oklahoma City, and now he'd been told about another inspector looking at tanks on one of Connex's farms. He'd instructed the security people to keep them out no matter who they worked for, specifically government inspectors. Some of his security people thought that odd, but it wasn't their job to question him.

"Ed, what is this shit about an inspector at the Hillrise yard? Didn't I make it clear they should not be allowed?"

"Well, sure, Henry. It was clear. This guy was told to leave, and the guards thought he did. He parked down the road a bit and doubled back on foot. The guards did like they were told, grabbed him and shoved him off the yard. He might've been hurt some, which means all hell's gonna break loose. That's their job to inspect these tanks, and we've just roughed one up. That whole group of bureaucratic assholes knows about Buck Howard, and now this. You better get on the horn with the governor and see if you can keep some order here. Otherwise, next time they come, they'll bring state troopers."

"Fuck."

"Yeah, 'fuck.' You can't cover this up anymore. You've got to get oil into those tanks, or somebody's going to jail."

"Well, genius, where do I get the money to put oil in those tanks?" Blackman was pissed at everybody. He had his plans all laid out, and now nothing was going the way it was supposed to. His eyes lit up at an idea. "Start a fire."

"'Start a fire'? What do you mean, 'start a fire'? Where?"

"At the Hillrise yard. Most of those tanks have some oil in them. You do this right, Ed, and that whole damn yard will go up. Make it look like arson, but stupid arson. We're going to blame this on the damned environmentalists. Figure this out, Ed, or we're done."

Ed shrugged. "It'll burn all right. Problem is, I'm not sure it'll stop. That's right next to that old refinery—our pipes connect to it. If there's a big fire, I'm guessing almost forty acres could go up. And just down the road about a mile is a residential area. It could burn for months. Jeez, Henry, maybe we should think about this."

"Listen, I do the thinkin'. This is no time to turn into a weaselly little coward. We need something that'll be so bad nobody'd suspect us of doing it deliberately. Otherwise, we both could end up in prison. They'll start looking real hard at Buck Howard. And where you were when he was killed."

"Henry, you're an asshole."

"Yeah, so what? Do what I told you."

Ed Black had always been a lowlife, either a common thug or sometimes doing really bad things. His association with Blackman put him in a new league. But the idea of torching a tank yard made him nervous. Blackman should know the risk, but maybe he'd forgotten. Once, back in the Fifties, they were working near a tank farm that exploded in Kansas. The heat was so intense metal melted a half-mile away. It burned for six months. All anyone could do was let it burn out. To do that on purpose in the middle of a city was almost beyond anything Ed would do. Almost.

There was risk of explosion from vapors, and Ed didn't know how big they might be. But he damned sure wasn't going to stay anywhere close after the fire started. To make sure it spread quickly, he would set it at three places in the yard. The oil in the ground would definitely burn, but it was harder than most people thought to get it lit. He brought gasoline for the ignitor. The pockets of vapor that might explode still worried him, but with the gasoline he thought the fires could be set from a distance and he could be out of the yard by the time they lit the oil. So he hoped.

Hillrise was the yard where Buck Howard had died, and it had the most leaks. Just being there gave Ed the creeps. He sent the security people to another yard ten miles away, telling them there had been a threat made against it. He poured a trail of gasoline, spending an hour getting everything ready. Once he was sure the escape route was clear, he lit all three gasoline trails, ran back to his truck, and drove out.

Ed heard a series of small explosions, then a huge one that almost shook his old truck off the road. He stopped and looked back to see a fireball, much bigger than he'd anticipated. It was the scariest thing he'd ever seen. *What the hell have we done?*

Reports were immediate. Hundreds of calls poured into the police and fire departments. People from Sunny Farm, a residential area, reported a huge fireball at the tank farm, and their windows were blown out. The lines were jammed.

Fifteen fire crews were scrambled. Police sent all available cars. Citywide emergency alarms used for tornado alerts were set off.

"What the hell's going on?" Chief "Sammy the Cop" Jackson entered the control center in the downtown headquarters building.

"We've got explosions and a fire at the tank farm on 33rd," a dispatcher replied, phone on her shoulder. "Callers say windows are blown out and you can see the flames from a mile away."

"Send out an emergency alert. Have all officers report."

"Chief," called an officer coming through the door, "you can see it from here. I was just out front. It looks like half the town is on fire."

Jackson went to a wall map, barking commands to dispatchers and ordering them to have officers block off roads, one of them being the interstate highway. Another explosion rocked police headquarters almost five miles from the fire.

"Shit. Did you feel that?"

A dispatcher screamed.

"Get me the mayor on the phone!" Jackson headed to his office. He had never been so scared.

The fire chief huddled with his officers. "That yard has been leaking for years, and now we're paying the price. Keep your men back two hundred yards, at least. We'll let that place burn, and I don't want *anyone* going into that yard. Tell them to start watering the surrounding areas best they can. Got it?"

He was so angry he could have kicked a puppy. He'd known the risks with those damned tank farms leaking but hadn't pushed to get them cleaned up. Damned oil people and their pet politicians, always saying they'd take care of it, that it was not a problem. And now a big part of his town was on fire. He headed to his car. He wanted to see it before he would let anyone risk their lives trying to put it out. He told himself again, no matter what the damned politicians said, he would let this mess burn out before he'd risk any men. He didn't care how many millions were at stake.

OK Journal

My View—Tommy Jacks

Two frustrating matters have us and the new, improved Oklahoma City Police Department at a loss.

One is the death more than a week ago of T.D. McFadden, which one of a thousand of you might have read about. If you did read, you may recall he'd fallen from grace as a state representative, was wrongly connected to shady deals, and fell for the wrong woman. If you knew all that, you might figure he put the small-caliber bullet hole in his own head without help. But Police Chief Tom Lawson isn't so sure.

Then there's a tougher case that has to do with a reporter from Tulsa who disappeared in Oklahoma City before McFadden was found dead. The two had nothing to do with each other, which is almost all anyone is sure about besides that Mathew Tomas hasn't been found. He checked into the Skirvin, attended a symposium, arranged a meeting with me and disappeared. The Skirvin said he never checked out, which happens, sometimes. The *Tulsa Herald*, where Tomas works as a political reporter, has not seen or heard a thing from or about him since.

So, here's where trust in your local journalists comes in. If you have anything to tell us, or the police, about these two men—even something you don't think amounts to much—call me, Lawson, the *Herald* or the *Sun*, or somebody. We can guarantee anonymity and that we'll take you seriously. 🐦

10
HELL ON EARTH

"Good evening. Chet Hunter, broadcasting live from Tulsa, Oklahoma, which tonight looks like a scene from biblical hell. Behind me are flames reaching hundreds of feet into the air after explosions rocked this community to its very core. In a town and a state built on oil, Tulsa is now threatened by the dangers of that flammable substance. We will have reports from the fire chief and the mayor on when they might have this disaster under control."

"How about that? Oklahoma's on national TV for looking like hell. Ought to be great for tourism." Vince was joking, but didn't seem in a good mood. Tommy and he sat in the capitol press room, watching a tiny black-and-white TV someone left there.

Tommy was downright angry. "That's Connex's tank farm. Think this is a coincidence?"

Vince shook his head. "I can't believe anyone would do that on purpose."

Tommy kept at it. He hated injustice and assholes, and this situation had both. "The tank farm where an inspector's body was found, the tank farm that by all accounts was the most contaminated in the state, the tank farm that, according to Fitzgerald, was listed as full while he personally observed it was mostly empty, now on fire. Come on, Vince. Blackman set it on fire. He doesn't give a shit who gets hurt or killed. It's all about him. He's trying to protect his own ass."

"Where's your proof?"

"Probably burning up with the oil."

They watched Hunter tilt his microphone toward the fire chief.

"Fire Chief Palmer, how long before you will have the fire under control?"

"We aren't sure. I know the people of Tulsa are tired of hearing that answer, but we just don't know."

"Can't you use foam and smother the fire?"

"The foam is a retardant and will reduce oxygen which, as we know, the fire needs to burn. But more important, it's a pollutant. This tank farm is right next to the Arkansas River, and the amount of foam needed could cause another environmental disaster. Once the flames burn down more, and we can use less foam, we might try that. But we don't know when that'll be."

Tommy shrugged. "If you don't know somethin', just say you don't know. Why can't politicians learn that?"

A hand reached in to give Hunter a piece of paper.

"Excuse me. My producer just handed me a press release from Connex, the company that owns this tank farm. Let me glance at this just a second. Once again, Chief Palmer, could I get you back in here? This press release from Connex says the company believes the fire at its tank farm has been deliberately set by an extreme environmentalist group called the 'Environmental Defense League.' Of course, this is only a press release, and we have no way of knowing if it is true. Do you have any evidence regarding this being an act of arson?"

"None at all. No one's been able to get into the yard yet. I have no

idea how they can make such a statement at this point. These types of fires are difficult to investigate. The temperatures are so high, nothing survives. Let me be clear that we haven't done any investigative work and have no statement regarding how it was started."

"Thank you, Chief Palmer."

"I've never even heard of the Environmental Defense League. Have you?" Vince frowned at the little TV.

"Nope. Wonder why Connex would say that. They're bound to know the next question will be, 'How do you know?' Do you think they have something?"

"Logic would say they do. And since the chief just made it clear no one could've examined the evidence on site to make that accusation, then the EDL, whoever the hell they are, made some kind of claim they did it." Vince had a well-developed sense of reporter's logic.

"I think we need to head to Tulsa. I think a news conference with Henry Blackman is about to happen."

Tommy called June at the *Journal* to tell her he and Vince wanted to go to Tulsa and look into the tank fire. She liked the idea but wanted to check with Fred and call back.

Soon the phone rang. "Press room. Jacks."

"Fred says go. I'll make reservations at the Mayo. We have a freelance photographer up there. Fred said he suspects Blackman will have a news conference, too, so your timing is perfect. Anyway, he wanted me to tell you and Vince, 'good job.' And," she added, "if you can, see if you can talk to Chet Hunter. Might be good for your column."

"Okay." Tommy wasn't sure about that. He was focused on Blackman and wanted to talk to Dick Fitzgerald, not cover TV personalities. Tommy hung up and called Fitzgerald.

"*Tulsa Herald.* Fitzgerald."

"This is Tommy. You the only one there?"

"Yeah, everyone's down at the fire. Mostly because the national TV networks are here. Big excitement at the circus."

"Yeah, I can imagine." Tommy told him their plans and arranged to meet him for a drink that night.

"*Mister Mayor, thank you for joining us. Do you have any information regarding this stunning statement from Connex that the fire burning behind us was set by a group of environmentalists?*"

"*All I know is what Connex said. I do know Connex and their president, Henry Blackman, and if they say something, you can take it to the bank. This is a disaster for our community and for Connex, one of our leading citizen companies. These crazy environmental people have just lost all sense. They convinced Nixon to start that EPA nonsense, and they won't give up until no business will be able to do anything, and then there'll be no jobs. I don't know how we survive if a tree has more rights than a human being.*"

Chet looked a bit stunned.

"*Well, yes, thank you Mister Mayor. We'll be right back.*"

"Chet just got introduced to one of our deep-thinking leaders," Vince observed.

They checked into the aging but classic Mayo, a landmark and host for many of the city's more famous visitors. There was something about an older building that gave it mystery and a sense of importance.

"Do you believe that an environmental group would set fire to that tank farm?" Tommy asked Dick while they slid into a booth in the Mayo's ornate bar.

"No way in hell. I've made calls. No one's heard of this 'Environmental Defense League.' There are groups with similar names, but none had anything to do with this fire. It's all Connex bullshit. They're blaming someone else before anyone can look for any evidence. How could an environmental group benefit from doing that?"

"Do you think it was an accident?" Vince asked Fitzgerald.

"Likely. That tank farm was a disaster waiting to happen. The leaks were bad enough, and Connex had almost no safety programs in place. You may not know this, but I'd interviewed the inspector who was found dead there, about four months before. Tomas asked me to do it as part of his research. That guy actually said that very thing to me— 'One of these days, that whole tank farm will go up in flames.' He told me no company was as lax as Connex when it came to safety. And with all that leaked oil, it wasn't going to take much to start something."

"Any way of telling if those tanks were empty or full when the fire started?"

"I'm no expert on that. I was helping Tomas because he was a friend, and most of what I know came from him. But based on that, I think trying to state how much oil was in the tank after a fire based on the length of time it burned or its intensity is just a guess." Fitzgerald shrugged and sipped his beer.

"Do you think Blackman could be involved?"

"My background's as a police beat reporter. I deal mostly with down-on-their-luck people doing things that under better circumstance they might not. Blackman is someone more or less on top of the world, but I think he's capable of all sorts of bad shit. I'd rather deal with my simple lowlifes than people like him. You interviewed him, Tommy. What did you think?"

"I've always wondered about souls and what they really are. And then I look someone like Blackman in the eye and see there's something missing. A key to being human, and it's not there. I don't think the man has a soul."

"So, we're in a fight with the devil?"

"Yeah. Or at the very least, one of his head demons."

They sipped their beers and shuddered. Doors would be locked that night.

OK Journal

My View—Tommy Jacks

Being reared in Oklahoma means sometime, somewhere, somehow you're going to go or get dragged into a church. Therein a man at least three times your age and maybe six times your size is going to flail and stomp and warn you that if you don't straighten up and follow any or all of his odd prescriptions, you will burn forever in hell. The message is clear: a life of sin means playing with fire.

And while you're sitting there trying not to look like you're checking your watch, that preacher will assure you that hell is a very hot place indeed. Its fire burns eternally, the Bible says.

It's impossible not to try to imagine what it looks like in the nether realm which some believe is where the Prince of Darkness rules.

Wonder no more. Just drive up to Tulsa, and you can fix your eyes upon it. The fire, as the preacher repeats, "is not quenched." And the devil feels close.

Near the same oil tank farm where the fire burns, the body of a state inspector was found some days ago. Even according to Connex, Henry Blackman's oil behemoth that put it on the banks of the Arkansas River, Buck Howard was told not to go poking around there. Now

Tulsa Police are trying to figure whether someone took some kind of bludgeon to Howard and pitched him down a riverbank. Now their chance to go back and reconnoiter the scene is getting the scorched-earth treatment.

Connex, however, says it knows who set the fire. That would be the Environmental Defense League, a violent and unprincipled group that will stop at nothing to halt progress and threaten the American way of life and pursuit of cash.

There's a problem, though. We have a source all the way up in Washington, working for an investigative agency that keeps track of the sorts of people and groups who might pull stunts like setting off oil tank farms. Asked about the Environmental Defense League, the source answered:

"Uh, nope. Can't say as we've ever come across or heard of that one. Ever."

Neither have Oklahoma City Police. Tulsa police and fire departments just shrugged.

But maybe we're barking up the wrong oil tank. Maybe we need to go ask the nearest fire-and-brimstone preacher. Maybe whoever put the torch to half of Tulsa will confess the devil made them do it. ❧

11
PLAN B AND PLAN Z

"Listen, Thorsten, be careful around Blackman. I know he's been our candidate there in Oklahoma. But I know that guy from his days in Kansas. He's dangerous."

"I don't understand, Mister Cook. Does this mean we aren't going to back him anymore?"

"That's not what I meant." *Why are all of the dentists and doctors who get involved in the cause such idiots?* thought Byron Cook, founder of the Freedom Branch Society and lifelong hater of the federal government. "That fire in Tulsa's going to be a problem for somebody, and my guess is it'll be Blackman. He's blaming some environmental group that no one's heard of. And why in hell would one set a fire like that, anyway? We just need to keep our distance from him until we know how this turns out."

"I don't mean to be disrespectful, sir," Daniels began to shout like he had a bad connection. "But someone has to defeat that commie Fillmore. Every time I think about him winning, I get so mad I can hardly talk. People like you and me will end up in jail if he wins."

Cook glared at the phone. *What!? Where do these people get these ideas?* "I agree, we don't want him to win, mostly because of government regulations people like him want to put in place. We need to fight for our freedoms, Thorsten, but we also need to be careful about getting too close to Blackman right now. Okay?"

"Yeah, I guess. I'm sure ready to fight. You give me the word, and me and my guns will be on the front lines quicker than you can say, 'God Bless America.'"

Cook sighed. *My god, these people really are nuts.* All he ever cared about was neutralizing the damn bureaucrats. He sure as hell didn't want to start a war. His idea of "good government" was one that didn't have the power to tell anyone anything. He believed in laws and enforcement, particularly for offenses like robbery or murder. But he wanted every goddamn bureaucrat from Washington to stay out of his state and his business. He also thought white men should have greater power, more than any other race and sure as hell more than women. The country had grown weak and no longer respected things that mattered, like honor and bravery. Now everyone wanted to be treated equally whether they earned it or not. That wasn't his world.

When the Freedom Branch Society started, he felt excited to associate with like-minded people in what felt to him like a good and just cause. As it grew, more people like Daniels joined, a bit crazy. Now it was mostly fanatics who believed things he didn't. And he wasn't sure he could control them.

He gathered himself and told Daniels, "I want you to make contact with the two other Republican primary guys, Clayton and Elliot. Tell them we're still open to backing them. Don't make any commitments. Just let 'em know that if they win, we'll give 'em support. Don't want Blackman to collapse and have those guys sayin' we didn't offer any help. I want to cover all our bases. Can you do that?"

"Sure. I'm headed into Tulsa this morning. Blackman's holding a news conference this afternoon, and I want to be there. I can try and see Elliot after that." Daniels sounded back to normal.

"Okay, that's good. But stay in the background. No pictures with Blackman, got it?"

"Yeah, I got it."

Tommy gave an update to June. "Looks like they've scheduled a news conference for one o'clock in the lobby of the Connex building just down the street. I've contacted the photographer, and he's going to be there. For now, we're going to the fire scene with Dick Fitzgerald from the *Herald*. If I run into one of those TV people, I'll see if they'll talk to me."

"Okay. Fred was real impressed with that fire chief. He suggested maybe you or Vince should try and meet with him. Of course, he's probably pretty busy, but it'd be good to get his input." June had the difficult task of trying to keep everyone moving in the same direction without taking sides. Fred was overly demanding, and she tried to make his requests sound like options, although he didn't mean them to be.

"Sure, we'll try. Anything else on the environmental group?"

"Nothing. There was some minister in Florida who made one of the national morning shows saying it was the end of the world because we've made God mad. But he also seemed to believe the fire was in Texas. So, he wasn't real credible." June chuckled but sounded like she had already put in a long day. And it was still morning.

On top of everything else, Tommy had heard two more

people had quit the *Journal,* and June and Fred were taking up the slack with no changes on the horizon. "Vince will call you and dictate his story. Try not to work too hard, okay? Talk to you later."

"You and Vince be careful. I woke up early this morning nervous, and I can't shake it—just be careful."

Tommy headed back to rejoin Vince in a coffee corner. "June says be careful. Said she woke up nervous and still feels that way. Funny, I didn't want to tell her, but I had the same feeling." He told him about the minister in Florida.

Vince laughed, but it was subdued. "You think Tomas is dead, don't you?" He spoke softly, as if exhibiting respect for the deceased.

Tommy lowered his head and nodded. "Yeah. I guess there could be some other explanation why he's missing, but I don't know what it is. So, without that, it must be he was killed weeks ago."

"It just doesn't make sense. He got his stuff from his room and left, and then he was killed? Or someone killed him and went to his hotel room and cleaned it out? And you know what else bothers me? Why was he going to tell you anything about Blackman, anyway? Look at us. We're friends, and we don't share many leads. Reporters protect their information until they're ready to go to print. He was working on this big story that's going to bring down one of the richest men in the state who's running for the Senate, and suddenly he bumps into you at an industry conference and he's ready to spill his guts? Come on, Tommy. Does that sound right?" Vince was frowning as if what he was saying was painful.

"No. It doesn't." Tommy felt shocked at himself that he

hadn't thought about it more critically. He wasn't sure about anything. "But what is it? We know he's missing. He hasn't been to work. He has a wife who, by what Fitzgerald said, is grieving like he's dead. No matter how you try to turn this, there are still big parts that don't make sense. And if he was just going to disappear, for whatever reason, why contact me at all?"

"Well, we're missing critical information," Vince said. "And I'm starting to think it has to do with Tomas. I have no proof, no evidence. But now I think he's still alive."

Tommy and Vince rode to the tank fire without saying anything about their earlier conversation to Dick Fitzgerald. They were now suspicious about everyone and everything.

Fitzgerald's beat-up old Dodge rattled through a series of small hills and tall trees. They could see the smoke from downtown and how high it loomed while they came closer. Once they topped the last hill, there it was. Tommy had never seen anything like what lay before him. The fire seemed alive. "It really is hell," he whispered. Its scale was so large the flames seemed almost staged.

"Should've seen it yesterday. I think it's about half that size now." Fitzgerald was the local talking to out-of-town visitors about the local attraction—*last year the trees were much more colorful; too bad you weren't here then.*

They could see fire crews using huge trucks in the distance like ones at airports when planes crash, shooting foam at the edges of the tanks on the east and north sides. The fire would almost roar when the foam hit, like the flames were complaining. Tommy estimated more than two hundred firefighters from Kansas, Arkansas, and Texas. That the fire could have been deliberately set seemed almost beyond belief.

Tommy spotted the now-famous fire chief, not far away. He signaled to Vince that he was going down the hill to talk to him.

"Chief Palmer, are you making progress?" *Stupid question,* Tommy thought, but he had to shout something.

"Nobody's supposed to be down here except firefighters. You'll need to leave." Chief Palmer had plenty to do without intruders making demands on his time.

"Sure. I'm with the *OK Journal.* Just wondered if that foam was working."

"Looks that way. We're only using it on the tank boundary farthest from the river, for now. But hopefully in a few more hours, we can expand that. Look, I'm glad to talk to the press when I have time, but it's dangerous down here, and you should leave."

"Okay. Thanks. Do you think someone set this fire?" Tommy sensed, based on the look from the chief, he might be pushing a little too much.

The chief sighed. "Most likely, but don't know who, and may never know. Based on some of the things we've seen, sure looks like it could be arson. Now you either go, or I'll have you tossed."

Tommy waved and headed up the hill. He got his quote. June would give him a big kiss. Reporters were annoying, persistent people, because sometimes that's what worked.

OK Journal

My View—Tommy Jacks

The oil giant Connex, run by Henry Blackman, who's all but sure to be the Republican to run for the Senate, is claiming that some group—which we still haven't found—ignited a life-size imitation of hell to prove how important it is to save our environment. As if that idea wasn't strange enough, Connex insists the authorities find these likely imaginary people and lock them up. That could mean an imaginary prison, but it's a cinch the cost will be in real money.

To sum up, a real crisis has been twisted beyond recognition and woven into a tapestry of doubt, misperceptions and maybe even lies, and then twisted one more time into a challenge to every sense of justice and truth. If we don't condemn and demand the apprehension and arrest of the Environmental Defense League, then we aren't real, red-blooded Oklahomans or Americans, because real patriots support the oil business, love its money, and want the government to stay out of both.

Right?

Fair enough. Let's show we have enough all-American courage to call Blackman's hand, then. Chase the EDL down to where it lives or doesn't live. Let's put the whole thing to a trial by fire.

Let's see who's telling the truth. 🐛

12
COVER UPS AND LIARS

The great lobby of Connex headquarters was packed with local and national news personnel. The company's tank farm fire brought attention to Oklahoma, although not the kind it wanted.

The conference had been scheduled for one in the afternoon; it was almost two. The crowd grew restless and pursued anyone who looked like they had something to do with the event. Finally, Henry Blackman entered the lobby trailed by an oddly even mix of assistants and goons.

Tommy whispered to Vince, "Looks more like the arrival of a Third World dictator than an Oklahoma businessman."

"You're surprised?"

Blackman tapped the microphone, causing it to thump and whine, and the crowd to cringe. "Glad to see so many media types. Must be good for the local economy, right, mayor?" He pointed to the mayor, grinning as if they shared a private joke. The mayor did not respond. "Okay, let's get started. We've suffered a huge tragedy at Connex, and the citizens of Tulsa have also suffered a monstrous crime against the community. These bastards at EDL have only one goal, and that is to cripple everything that America stands for. They want to take away our freedoms and turn us against one another. We are absolutely shocked that they have attacked our company. We are proud of our safety record and our careful management of these vital resources. The production and transportation of oil is critical to our state and our nation, and these environmental nuts are trying to disrupt that whole operation. And why? Because they hate our way of life and our great country. As president of Connex, I will assure you we will fight with every resource at our disposal to protect our company, our industry, our state and our nation against these vicious attacks by these evil instigators. It is one of the reasons I am running for the U.S. Senate— to bring good Oklahoma common sense to our nation's capital, and to fight against these extremists who want to destroy our way of life."

Blackman paused, and the group started shouting questions. He held up his hand. "Just one minute. I want to say something about this fire, and then I'll take a few questions. First, I want to congratulate our great fire chief and his men in their heroic effort to contain this disaster. We've been in constant communication with the chief, and he has our one hundred percent support in his efforts to contain the damage of this fire. Also, I want to explain that within a very short amount of time after the fire started, we found a blank manila envelope at our front desk. We don't know how it got there, and nobody at Connex saw who put it there. Inside was a typed letter from this extreme group, the 'Environmental Defense League.' The group claimed responsibility for the fire. They demanded we admit our 'guilt' in polluting and also that I drop out of the Senate race, or they would act again against one of our other fields. We do not know who these people are, but we take their threat seriously. We immediately placed greater security around all our assets. We are cooperating with the authorities to identify the people who are threatening our company and our state. Regarding their charge that we pollute—that's nonsense. We've operated a safe company ever since we started, and annually receive awards for our concern for the environment. These people at EDL are liars. And there's no way in hell these bastards would force me to drop out of the Senate race. I'm staying in to fight these very people, and I will not be intimidated. Questions?"

"Can we get a copy of the letter EDL sent?"

"I believe we've given everything to Police Chief Jackson." Blackman looked to Ed Black, who nodded. "So, you'll have to ask the police chief about that."

Vince raised his hand. "There was a state tank inspector found dead on that same tank farm not long ago. Do you believe this fire has anything to do with his death?"

"What a stupid question. That man's death was an accident. You people are always trying to stir something up without any facts to support your crazy ideas. This news conference is over." Blackman gave Vince a hard glower and left the lobby with his groupies.

The TV people also sent Vince plenty of dirty looks. It had taken them thirty minutes to set up, they had waited an hour, and just like that the dumb newspaper guy had run off the star of the show. They really didn't care what Blackman said. They just wanted footage.

"I don't think Blackman likes you." Tommy smiled, moving away.

"Tommy, it's Mathew Tomas. I'm in Tulsa. I need to talk to you."

Tommy almost dropped the receiver, feeling his way backward onto the hotel-room bed. He felt suddenly dizzy. "My god, where are you? Where've you been?"

"I know this is all screwed up, but there's a reason. I read your column about me and realized I've really messed up. I need your help."

Tommy's mind raced. "Okay. Where do we meet?"

"Centennial Park on Sixth. Meet me at the corner of Sixth and Peoria."

"When?"

"An hour."

Tommy felt confused and conflicted. Should he call Dick Fitzgerald or Vince? He decided against Dick—he wasn't yet sure about him. He called Vince's room and told him to meet him in the lobby.

"What's the mystery?"

"You're not going to believe this, but Mathew Tomas just called me. He wants to meet."

Vince was stunned. "My god. Where has he been?"

"Don't know yet. I guess I'm nervous about it. Maybe you could follow me just to make sure he's not some kind of insane killer or something."

Vince shook his head. "Look, if there's a risk, you shouldn't meet him. We should call the police and let them take care of it."

Tommy thought a moment. "On the other hand, this could be one hell of a story. It has to be something, right? And even if it makes me nervous, I really don't think he's dangerous. Still, I'd feel better if someone was watching when I meet him."

"Yeah, I guess. If he does kill you, I'll still have time to run."

Vince wasn't trying to be funny.

Tommy sighed. "Thanks. Meet back here in thirty minutes."

Tommy couldn't see Vince as he approached Sixth along Peoria, which meant either he was much better at this tailing business than he let on, or he'd gone back to the hotel. He crossed Peoria and to the park. Its trails circled a lake and benches were everywhere. But, no Matt. Tommy felt annoyed. Did the guy just stand him up again? Just as he wondered whether to leave, he saw him walking from the far side.

"Sorry. Had to take a bus, and it let me out on the wrong side. Let's go sit." Tomas kept looking around on their way to a bench off the path. "I owe you a full explanation, but first let me say that what I wanted to tell you about Blackman is more important than anything, especially now. I'm absolutely sure his people set that fire." His tone was serious and urgent.

The intensity Tommy saw in him before seemed the same, at least. "Why did you skip out on me?"

"I was headed down to see you and I spotted someone I didn't want to see, and who I didn't want to see me. That wasn't about Connex, but it involves some bad people. I panicked. I got my stuff and left out the back."

"Okay, just start over. Who did you see, and why were you scared?"

Matt swallowed. "This is hard. I know everyone thinks it had to do with what I was going to tell you about Blackman and Connex. But it didn't. See, I'm no angel. And I may have broken the law. And the person I was avoiding was part of that. I'm embarrassed because I'm not the noble journalist everyone thought. I don't know how to fix this."

Tommy gulped down his annoyance. "Nice speech. But it doesn't answer my questions."

Matt sighed. "My cousin. His name's Chuck Branson."

Tommy mind was spinning. So, he *did* see Chuck at the hotel. He would not have guessed a connection to Matt. "All right. But why did seeing him scare you?"

Matt wrung his hands. "I'd been helping him some over the last year or so. He'd send packages to my house, and I'd deliver them to a guy who ran a car lot up here. I knew, because it was Chuck, that it had to be something illegal. But he was paying me, and I needed it. So I just kept delivering the packages. Dick Fitzgerald, who's our police beat reporter and my friend, told me that he'd met the police beat reporter for the *OK Journal,* and I told him he was my cousin. After he heard Chuck had quit and was suspected of crimes in Oklahoma City, he told me. I knew right then I'd wind up in trouble sooner or later. Then another package arrived. I rented a storage locker at the bus station, put it there and waited. Nothing happened, so I just went on about my life. When I saw Chuck at the hotel, I knew he was looking for me. And I figured if he thought I'd crossed him, he'd kill me, family or not. So, I ran."

"Where did you go?"

"Got on a bus and went to Sand Springs. My cousin let me stay with him, no questions asked. The only person I told was my wife, and I let her know she had to play dumb. Then I read your column about me. I knew I had to fix things."

"People are looking for Chuck. Especially the feds."

Matt shuddered. "I don't know what was in that last package. If it was money, it could be a lot."

Tommy chuckled. He couldn't help it. He liked Mathew Tomas. "Well, I'll have to think about all this. I do know that unless you want to hide for the rest of your life, you'll have to talk to the police and then deal with the consequences."

"Yeah. I'm ready for that. I just don't want to get killed."

"I know the perfect lawyer when the time comes. Now—tell me, what were you going to say to me at the Skirvin."

"I knew the inspector who got killed. In fact, I'd gone out to the tank farm that night. I was supposed to meet him. He'd already given me documents that showed those tanks were empty. And pages out of the stock offering, saying they were full. That alone meant Connex had more than a million dollars less in oil value than it said on the stock filing. If that's true for all their tank farms, you just multiply that. And he gave me documents showing how unsafe the yards were—they didn't even do the minimum. He had more specifics to show me that night. I knew he'd been murdered. But I backed off the story. I wondered whether they knew he'd talked to me. I had his documentation, but no corroborating witness anymore." He raised his eyes, at last, to look at Tommy. "Then I started reading your columns. I decided that when I was in Oklahoma City, I would see what you thought about how to pursue the story. Then I saw Chuck. And I ran."

What a strange world we live in, Tommy thought. He didn't know how much of it was true or useful, but what Matt told him meant the investigative team had a lot more meat to tear into. They no longer needed to find the lost journalist. Their quest was to defeat the devil.

Tommy spotted Vince and waved him over. He approached reluctantly.

"I think I see a Pulitzer in your future." Tommy tried out his best mischievous smile.

OK Journal

My View—Tommy Jacks

Because we live in Oklahoma and it's summer, we can guarantee a storm. We can't say how big or how strong it will be. But one is brewing.

Connex says it got a letter from the Environmental Defense League, who Henry Blackman, the oil giant's owner, claims set the fire. Darn the luck, we can't see it because he handed it to Tulsa Police. And Blackman and all the geniuses at Connex didn't even so much as copy it out in crayon. But hey, we can take his word for what it says, to wit: the EDL wants Connex to admit all the polluting it's done and for Blackman to drop out of next year's race for the U.S. Senate seat Rick Butler's kept lukewarm in the meantime.

The EDL only sounds like ordinary Democrats on those accounts. Also, Blackman doesn't seem to want anyone to notice that he's the only one who insists the EDL—which no one, not even the feds, has been able to turn up or put any names or faces to—is responsible for the flaming catastrophe on the west bank of the Arkansas. Nor does he seem interested in countering the argument that it makes no sense that a group with a philosophy presumptively like the EDL's would set off so much as a bottle rocket to make its point. And it doesn't matter to him that the only evidence that says they did, came from his hands, as in: not from anyone institutionally trained to investigate criminal activity.

But this is Oklahoma. The storms here break forth without warning, and they spare no one. ❦

13

LEGAL EAGLES AND REDEMPTION

"Mister Tomas, I've been thinkin' about what you've told me."

"Please," Matt told Joe Louongo, "just call me Matt."

"Sure, why the fuck not? Look, Matt, you've got choices to make. Here's the way I see it: you can spill your guts and maybe make a deal with the DA—not so sure about the feds—so maybe you only serve a little time, or maybe none. Or you can just ignore the whole thing, and more than likely they'll never know you screwed up." Louongo shrugged, hands spread atop his desk. He was brutally honest, but not always clear.

"I guess I don't follow."

Louongo nodded evenly. "I'm glad to explain. You know, every day some jackass sends somethin' through the mail that's not legal. The dumbass mailman delivers it and gets paid to do that. Nobody ever arrests the mailman, do they? Just the same way, you were just a delivery guy. Your cousin paid you for the service, but you didn't know what was in those packages. So, it's like you and the mailman are the same—innocent. The problem is, if you go to the great minds who run the legal system and tell them you might've had an idea there was something fishy goin' on, they'll be forced to figure out some way to charge you with somethin'. Now the problem you have is that last package. You don't know what's in it, right?"

"Right."

"So, if that package was destroyed, then there's no way you could know what your cousin was asking you to deliver. But here's the rub. That might be destroying evidence. So, doing that could be a crime. Of course, you've destroyed the evidence, so—no crime. Get it?"

Matt didn't really, but said, "It could be a lot of money."

"Yeah. But if you keep it, you probably *have* committed a crime. Burn the money, no crime. Now, of course, this all assumes your cousin doesn't want whatever was in the package back and won't be pissed if you burn it."

"Yeah." Matt cleared his throat. "He could get real angry about that. He's not a nice person."

"Then it might be better to go with 'Plan B.' You and me go to the feds and, as an act of lawfulness, you give them the last package. You tell them your cousin has threatened you, and you need their protection. You tell them everything you know about your cousin, which is almost nothing but maybe the name of the car dealer. They forgive you for not coming forward sooner because they really don't care, and they agree to no charges. And they'll provide you and your family protection for a while. Everybody's happy."

"You seem to be saying I really didn't commit a crime."

Louongo grimaced. "Well, you did, sort of, but not really. You knew that most likely what you were delivering was not legal. But since you never looked and didn't know for sure, you can claim innocence. They can say your cousin wouldn't have paid as much as he did unless he knew it was illegal, but you can counter that he paid you like that because you're family and he knew you needed the money. You may have thought your cousin was a crook, but because you didn't know anything specific, you had no responsibility to tell authorities anything. So, no crime. The only crime potential is that last package. But you just tell them you didn't turn it in sooner because you were afraid of your cousin and what he might do. I don't think any of your choices involve you being charged with anything—unless, of course, you keep the last bundle and spend it, smoke it, snort it, or whatever."

Ray addressed the investigative group. "I met with Mister Gilmore and Mister Anderson and discussed the documents Tommy and Vince were given. We all think they supply substantial evidence that Connex has committed financial fraud. There appears to be no question they falsified their filing for a stock offering and have gone to great lengths to cover that up. Vince, tell us what happened when you contacted the oil commission."

Vince cleared his throat. "I hand-delivered copies of the inspection reports on state oil commission forms to the commission's offices at the capitol. I met with their in-house attorney, who informed me they didn't have any such forms in their files and could only assume these were forgeries. They were openly hostile to any questions. Minutes after I returned to the *Journal* I got a call from Connex's attorney, Gary Hillman of Tulsa. He told me if we ran a story based on those documents, Connex would sue. He said the damage we could do with these 'lies' would be in the millions. My gut says everyone

I talked to overreacted. They were nervous. I think there's no doubt they're real." He shrugged.

Ray nodded. "The legal people at both papers say without more proof or some corroboration, we don't have enough to go to print. That isn't surprising. But we're stirring the pot, and something will come our way if we keep digging. On the 'good news' front, Robbie has decided, based on this information, he will not endorse Blackman. That's a victory for us."

If it was, it felt hollow. They still had nothing to publish.

Tommy spoke up. "We're still months away from the primary, and Blackman's still the favorite. Without the *Sun's* endorsement, he's a wounded general election candidate. If we keep digging, we'll come up with more. That fire chief in Tulsa is an honest guy. He'll find out how the fire was set, and I believe Blackman's goons did it. This guy has too many loose ends for something not to break."

Ray stood. "Tommy and Vince are right. Let's keep digging. Janet, I want you to follow up with the coroner's office in Tulsa. They still haven't released a cause of death for Buck Howard. Vince, work with Dick and try to get answers from Tulsa police about that. Find out who's in charge of the investigation. Get them in the paper, get some quotes. We need to increase the pressure."

Fire Chief Palmer held up his hand for quiet from the small contingent of newspaper and TV people gathered for the update at the main fire station. His routine was to give an estimate of the percentage of the fire under control and go over new information, if any. Most news outlets had stopped attending. Dick Fitzgerald made it to every one.

"A little bit more news today," Palmer began. "First, we think we have it about seventy percent contained with the help of last night's rain. We brought in a new foam truck from Oklahoma City this morning, and we should be close to full containment by Friday. In another matter, we were notified by the Baptist church located near the fire zone that there were possibly two eyewitnesses to the setting of the fire."

Everyone looked up.

"The church helps out homeless people, a lot of them from a camp by the river. On the night of the fire, two such men were headed to the church and stopped for a smoke out by the tank farm. While they were there, they say they saw a truck enter the yard and one man get out. They couldn't tell what he did, but it was something around one of the biggest tanks. They thought he used big gasoline cans. They figured he was a Connex person, so they kept still."

Everyone leaned in, scribbling furiously.

"They said it was about forty minutes before the guy walked back to his truck and left the yard. They got ready to leave and heard an explosion. They ran off toward the church and didn't tell anyone. Eventually they told the minister what they saw. He thought they could help find who set the fire. So, the minister called us, and they're in protective custody. They have given us a description of the truck and the man they saw. They also have identified precisely where the man was in the tank farm. That will help us to focus our investigation. They're working with a police sketch artist to come up with an image of the man so police can try and locate him. Questions?"

Hell yes, there were questions. Everybody started shouting

at once. The fire chief pointed to the most attractive woman in the front—why not?

"Can you give us a general description of the man?"

"They said he was some distance off, and these guys are not trained observers. So the descriptions are a work in progress. But I think with the help of the police artist, we'll end up with something useful. So, give us a day or two on that."

"Did those guys see any Connex guards around when that guy was there?" That came from Dick.

"They said on that night the yard was empty until the pick-up guy showed up."

"Any chance that the pickup guy was a Connex person?"

"We can't say. The witnesses did say the guy seemed to know his way around."

"You said they waited to tell anyone. Do you know why?"

"There was a second blast—a big one—and it knocked them to the ground and damaged their eardrums. Neither of them could hear for a couple of days. They told the minister that they wrote notes to each other and agreed to keep quiet because they thought God had punished them by making them deaf because they were drinking a bottle of wine while they watched the man in the yard. They feared God might destroy the world because of them."

OK Journal

My View—Tommy Jacks

"But the day of the Lord shall come . . . and the elements shall melt with fervent heat, the earth also and the works that are therein shall be burned up."—2 Peter 3:10

According to the chief of the Tulsa Fire Department, a couple of down-and-outers in his town at least know the Bible. They're regular customers at a mission run by Baptists and pay for prized hot meals with attention to sermons.

The Baptists are big on spreading the Word to audiences like them. Their lessons regularly refer to parts that have a lot to do with fire and judgment.

How pertinent.

For these two guys, whose persons and names are being kept out of reach for a list of reasons we can't help but grudgingly agree with, the Baptists' sermons for about a couple of days after the Connex tank farm fire started fell on clinically, albeit temporarily deaf ears.

The two were that close when the big boom went off.

Their stories check out. The police take them at their word that they'd pulled up that night near the tank farm to polish off a bottle and share a smoke before heading out to take in that night's sermon.

They said the blast knocked them down and deafened them. And they may have seen whoever set it.

Of course, they weren't familiar with the man who they say pulled a pickup into the yard, did something with military-style fuel cans, and left. They didn't see anything that connected him to anyone, whether a phantom environmental group that no one but Henry Blackman of Connex seems to know about, or Connex itself. But they're helping police work on it.

And it's hard not to wonder what Blackman's feeling or thinking, or how much expensive whiskey he's going through to drown out the fervent heat building up around the works he's put on this earth.

The first thing to melt will be the one that is least able to stand a slight rise in temperature: the so-called Environmental Defense League, Blackman's tree-huggers who aren't there.

To put a point on it: the EDL does not exist.

The heat is getting fervent. What's left after everything Blackman did and said melts? ❧

14
SHOW BIZ MEETS NEWS BIZ

Tommy's interviews on *Oklahoma AM* since his Blackman blowup had been successful in the sense that there hadn't been any mistakes. Still, they were bland. "Complete crap," the show's producer called them.

He was never pleased, but always had suggestions. "Listen, Tommy, we don't have the time or the need to be getting deep into whatever the guest might be talking about. We just want one good line. Get the person to say something our audience can remember, or something newsy. This isn't a story for the paper. This is live TV. Get to the point quicker."

That led Tommy to ask himself, "Why the hell are you doing this?" He didn't have a good quick answer. His first job was to bring stories to his readers in five hundred words or less. He knew newspapers were no longer the place for long-form journalism. But no one seemed interested in details anymore. He loved details.

The producer wanted everything cut down to the best few minutes of air time. Ignore all else; nobody's interested. Even if Fred and June were less annoying, they wanted everything to be "hard-hitting" and "to-the-point." Paper and ink cost money; keep it right, bright, and tight. News now was all about highlights. Could anyone be informed with just headlines?

And here he was, doing TV interviews with politicians with canned answers to obvious questions. Everyone was playing a game—including Tommy.

"You look deep in thought." Tracy found him sitting in the TV studio break room.

"Probably too *much* thought. According to the producer, thought is not required." Tommy was whining.

"Don't listen to that little creep. He's only smart this week. Next week he could be gone. Nothing lasts long in this business."

"That might be part of the problem. I'm not sure I fit in the TV world."

"Hey, you're doing great."

He shook his head. "I get that it's TV, and interviews can only go a few minutes. But I feel like I'm contributing to the dumbness of the audience with this charade like we're covering some issue when all we do is highlights."

Tracy smiled. "Yeah. We let a lot of stuff slide to get to the next commercial. Even if you write that essay that completely covers a subject and get it into print, very few would read it. Not much demand for in-depth thought. And there's the competition for the audience. But your column's read by more people in one day than academic bestsellers or in-depth essays. You're good at what you do. Don't fight it so much."

Tommy looked at the beautiful Tracy, realizing what a great friend she was. And it was accidental. Life was strange and wonderful. "I know. Things are going great for me and I'm still moody. Patsy says I'm a sourpuss."

"She can say that because she loves you. You're a thinker, Tommy. Thinkers are always moody. You're not wrong about TV. It's superficial and usually useless as a news source. Do your best to change that. Don't listen to the producer; he has no idea. Conduct those interviews with one goal: to get the guest to tell you *something*. Get to understand the person. Don't be afraid to ask that tough question. Your best interview by far was Blackman. You made him mad, and he stormed off. That's great TV. You can't alienate your guests, but you can't be their friend, either. You understand how to interview people. Use those skills."

Pep talk, *again*. "Thanks, Mom."

"Our guest this morning is Howard Fillmore, president of Corinthian Oklahoma College and Democratic candidate for the U.S. Senate. Thanks for joining us today, Doctor Fillmore."

"My pleasure, Tommy."

"Some people have called you a communist and a liberal college professor. Can you be elected in conservative Oklahoma with those labels?"

Fillmore smiled. "Not if the people believe they're true. Sure, I lean toward liberal politics. But so do many of Oklahoma's politicians because they and I care about the people. I care about good jobs, good schools, Social Security, and a health care system that doesn't exclude much of our people. Caring like that doesn't make anyone a communist. I think many will agree with my positions. But if they only listen to hysterical name-calling by some who support my opponents, they probably won't vote for me. Labels are just a way of avoiding issues that matter. I'm going to stick with an agenda for all voters in this state, not just a few."

"You're currently leading in the few polls that have been

conducted for the Democratic primary. Henry Blackman is currently leading in the Republican polls. If you win, you may be running against him. Do you think the fire in Tulsa at one of his company's tank farms is a political issue?"

"Based on what I know, I'd say no. We complain all the time about only professional politicians running for office, but when someone like Blackman, a businessman, runs, we examine every aspect of his life. That of course includes his business. Connex is a huge company, and it's hard for a businessman to not have some baggage. I'm more than willing to give Mister Blackman the benefit of the doubt until it's proven otherwise."

"Some people say you're an environmentalist, which is right up there with 'communist' for them. Do you think that there are circumstances where an environmentalist group could justify the kind of action the EDL group has been accused of committing?"

"Easy answer: no. The 'environmentalist' label is another being used in a derogatory way. I'm concerned about the environment, which means clean air and water, control over toxic chemicals, and smart regulations. But that doesn't mean I think trees are more important than people. Still, I believe it's part of a government's responsibility to protect the environment for future generations. I also know the matter can become controversial. We have to be able to discuss these issues and come up with what is best for all concerned."

"Thank you, Doctor Fillmore, for joining us this morning."

Tommy headed to the press room in the state capitol. Seemed like it had been a long time since he had been in his favorite workplace.

"Hey, Mister TV Star. Long time, no see." Bart gave a friendly wave to Tommy. Bart was a security guard at the capitol who had made Tommy, on his first day at the capitol, jump through imaginary hoops to get into the press gallery. That strange beginning had led to a terrific friendship.

"Missed your charming face. What's goin' on?"

Bart grinned casually. "Oh, there was that fistfight at the oil and gas offices the other day. Real cops came out. Seems some assistant or something slugged his boss and got taken into custody. Broke his boss's nose. So much for a happy workplace. Gail asks about you all the time. Says she thinks you've turned into a snob, but she doesn't mean it."

Fistfight? Tommy thought, but didn't pursue it. Bart tended to turn sensitive when interrogated. He stuck to the subject of Gail Collins, top assistant for former Senator, now Governor Bud Evans. "I need to stop by and see her," Tommy agreed. She had worked with Tommy's first true love and had been very supportive after she was killed. He went to another subject. "How's Larry doing at Risso's?"

"He complains all the time how business is bad. When the legislature's not in session, I guess it is. But I think he makes out okay. Every time I see him, he asks me about you. He thinks you've turned into a TV snob, too." He grinned again.

"No way. Even TV stars need pizza and beer." Tommy waved on his way upstairs to the governor's office to say hi to Gail. She was out, so he left a note and went to the press room.

"Hey, Vince. You hiding from Fred?"

"I know you claim ownership of the press room, but I've been told you have to share."

"Yeah, by who?"

"June. And remember she has a gun in her desk."

"Good enough for me. You just hanging out or got somethin' goin' on?"

"Had an appointment with Walter Jefferson, chairman of the Corporation Commission. Got a tip there was a fight the other day in the Oil and Gas Division between Lyles, who runs that department, and a clerk. Don't have the clerk's name yet. Anyway, I guess the clerk broke Lyles's nose, and they called Oklahoma City PD. The clerk got arrested. Still don't have a police beat reporter, so June told me to follow up. Whoever left the tip didn't leave a name. So I started off at the police department, and guess what? It never happened."

Tommy looked at him sideways. "What do you mean? I just saw Bart, and he told me about it. Said the police came and took some guy away."

Vince shrugged. "The police say nothing ever happened, and they never arrested anyone at the state capitol on or about that time. Said someone must've lied to me. So I call the Corporation Commission and asked to speak to the guy in charge. And this is weird—they put me right through to Jefferson. He was real polite and said he wasn't aware of any fights and would have to get back to me. I asked if he could meet with me if I came down. He said yes, but I could tell he didn't want to. Now I show up, and he's gone for the day. I asked for someone else and got the cold shoulder."

Tommy took a seat. "You know Buck Howard worked for the Oil and Gas Division, right? We need to find out about this fight."

"How do we go about that?"

"The governor's in. Let's go see him." Vince gave Tommy an

"I hope you know what you're doing" look. Tommy smiled. "I know his assistant. She'll get us in."

The governor led Tommy and Vince into his office. "This is a new approach. Drop-in reporters, working in pairs. Must confess, Tommy—feels like a sneak attack." Governor Evans was indeed a politician, but one of the better ones.

"Sorry to just drop in. We have a quick question. The other day there was a fight in the Corporation Commission. We got an anonymous tip on it, plus one of the security guards I know mentioned it. Vince was checking it out, and now everyone tells us it never happened. Do you know about this?"

Evans looked at Tommy. It seemed clear he was thinking. "I heard about the fight, and that an employee was arrested for hitting his boss. How can anyone say it didn't happen?"

Tommy shrugged. "Vince had an appointment with Jefferson to discuss it, but he left for the day."

The governor dialed his phone. "Jefferson, I've got a couple of reporters in my office. They are asking about the fistfight the other day and the guy who was arrested. Seems the city police say it didn't happen. Do you know why?" The governor listened. He listened for some time, then hung up and cleared his throat. "This has to be off the record until I can get all the facts. Jefferson called police after the clerk was arrested and told them that Lyles, the guy's boss, wouldn't file charges, and that the state wanted the clerk released. He was never charged. And he has since disappeared."

"You should know this could have something to do with Connex and Henry Blackman. I trust you, governor, but I can't stay off the record for long."

The governor did not look pleased.

15

BAD NEWS AND OTHER NEWS

Gary Hillman sat in front of Henry Blackman's huge desk. "I don't believe you have much of a choice, Henry. Either pull the stock offering, or the SEC will force you to. If they file in court to do that, you may never be able to put together another offering."

"Fuck. What kind of goddamn lawyer are you? You need to get this fixed. I need that money now!" The veins in Henry's neck were bulging.

"Not sure yelling at me will do any good. This fire, and the publicity it's generated, is considered an extraordinary event. By law the stock offering has to be delayed until there's time to assess the damage to the company and, therefore, the accuracy of the filing documents. It's not about me or you."

"Fuck." Henry got up, stalked to a credenza, poured some whiskey and chugged it. He was not a day drinker, but lately the stuff seemed necessary. In a calmer voice he asked, "How do we fix this?"

"My guess, it'll take six months or longer, and we'll have to file a whole new set of documents. There'll be due diligence all over again. Could be over a year." He took a deep breath. "I've been your attorney for years, and you've mostly just barked at me, but you should know my firm is one of the best in the

Southwest when it comes to corporate bankruptcy. You can try and hide your problems and run the risk of everything collapsing, or you can fight for the company in bankruptcy court and maybe keep things afloat." Hillman really didn't care what Henry did.

"Bankruptcy. Isn't that just great? No more money, no more company, everything run by fuckin' lawyers. No more Senate race—that goddamn commie Fillmore will probably win. Fuck!" Henry glared at Hillman like he could kill him. The pause lasted an uncomfortable moment before Henry bellowed, "Get the fuck out of here, now!" Hillman quickly left.

Bankruptcy court. Every day for the next five years he would be told what to do by some piss-ant attorneys, and that would amount to kissin' up to some moron judge. All the time, legal vultures would drain him dry with fees and more fees. He had to figure out a way to keep everything going; he had to think of an angle. He was going to run for Senate and win. Senator Henry Blackman—try to fuck with him then! Damned lawyers—that's how he got into this mess, with them always saying somethin' had to be a certain way even if it wasn't what he wanted. He wasn't going to listen anymore.

He headed to his desk and grabbed the phone. "Ed, you asshole! I need to get shit-faced drunk so I can think straight—want to join me?"

"Sure, why the fuck not?"

Henry craved water. He stumbled into the bathroom and cupped his hands to receive the wonderful liquid. He'd given up heavy drinking years ago as a concession to age, and now he remembered that his behavior of years ago would likely kill him now. He seemed to be in a hotel room—couldn't recall much after he and Ed got started.

Out of that fog and aches from head to toe, he remembered his plan. It came in a drunken flash, while he berated Ed for being so stupid. He realized his solution was to sell the company. And only one person he knew could bail him out in time: that crazy Byron Cook.

Sure, Connex was cash-poor and about to default on massive loans. But it owned vast oil reserves, potentially worth millions. Selling it crossed his mind before, but he didn't figure he had time to put the company on the market. Besides, he'd have to file for bankruptcy, and he refused that idea. But Cook could do the deal right away.

Henry and Ed worked for Cook years ago when they were all younger. They helped him bust up talk about a union in his first oil company. Cook hated the idea of unions and expected his people to do as told without dissent. He had rig crews in a prime field along the Kansas-Oklahoma border who'd hit a run of bad luck—a couple of roustabouts killed in accidents. A leader emerged and started to organize a fight for safer working conditions. It was like waving a red flag at a bull. Cook hired Henry and Ed to spread the word that there would be no union in his company. The organizer suffered an accident. He died, and so did talk of unionizing.

Police investigated and determined no foul play. Henry knew the truth. It wasn't an accident.

Cook Oil and Gas became one of the most successful exploration companies in the Kansas-Oklahoma region, and Byron Cook became one of the richest men in the nation. He also gained a reputation as a ruthless, violent man who would do anything to succeed. Few challenged the man called—behind his back—Crazy Cook.

As if in testimony to that nickname, he started donating to every far-right political group that advocated a freedom-from-government agenda. The only people who ever challenged Crazy Cook were federal bureaucrats. To answer them, he formed the Freedom Branch Society with a few of his like-minded fellow millionaire oilmen who wanted government to stay out of their business. Together they consolidated control over most state government bureaucracies that regulated oil and gas. The states depended on taxes extracted along with the oil. That dependence, and bribes, led to regulations that hardly interfered with drilling for more oil and were rarely enforced. The federal government, on the other hand, saw a business being allowed to pollute. Battle lines were drawn. Cook's stated goal was freedom from unnecessary regulation. It could just as easily have been the overthrow of the federal government.

Henry took a shower and discovered he was in the penthouse at the Mayo. He wondered how he got there and where Ed might be, although he really didn't care. He put on his yesterday clothes and left without checking out—he'd either already paid or they'd bill him. He was in a hurry. Even with a massive headache, he had a plan.

Tommy sat in the press room, sipping coffee and thinking about his evening with Patsy. He grinned. He was at work so early because she had stayed the night and got up at dawn to get ready for work. Out of a sense of guilt, he got up, too, and started his day with a smile on his face. He jumped when the phone rang.

"Press room. Jacks."

"Tommy, I'm at Denny's. How about breakfast, papers, and a little conversation?" The line went dead before he could answer. Albright was mostly annoying. But he immediately got up and left, looking forward to meeting up with his mentor.

Denny's was, as usual, hectic. He was surprised to find the whole group in the corner booth—Taylor Albright, Nathan Oliver, Max Jones, and Joe Louongo. The band of old was together again. Tommy could not help smiling.

"Well, shit, look who's here. The world-famous TV interviewer, Tommy Jacks. My god—move over, guys. Let the star have a seat." Albright smiled, still with that edge to his voice that conveyed more than his words.

Tommy shook Nathan's and Max's hands—always be polite to deadly men—and gave a little wave to Louongo's direction. "You've returned just to check up on me? Make sure I'm doing what I'm supposed to be doing?"

"Sure. Tell me what's goin' on with the Senate race. Who do you think's goin' to win?"

Tommy had missed Albright's no-bullshit approach to conversation. No how ya doin', no how's your dad, how's Tracy—just right to the point: tell me the latest. "Fillmore and Blackman look like sure winners in the primaries, mostly due to no real effort by their opponents. So the focus has already shifted to the general election. There the real news is Blackman and whatever's going on with Connex. The fire in Tulsa, the claim it was set by some group nobody can find, and Blackman's handling of the whole mess could hurt him. So, I'd guess Howard

Fillmore is feeling pretty good. Is that why you're here—to decide whether you'll run his campaign?"

"Once a nosy reporter, always a nosy reporter. I hear the *Sun*'s not going to endorse anyone. You think that's true?" Albright was mining for information.

Tommy admired Albright's tactics. "You'd have to ask Robbie Gilmore. But my guess is that if the *Sun* doesn't endorse anyone, that's due to Blackman's handling of the fire and some of his recent comments to the press. He's lost his temper in several interviews, including one with me. Not getting the *Sun*'s endorsement will hurt. But at this point in the election, most voters aren't paying attention. So his behavior might not be important now. Once the general election begins, it's a different story."

"You think Fillmore can win in backward Oklahoma?"

"I think so. Now, of course, if he has an out-of-state campaign manager who refers to his beloved home state as 'backward,' that can make things a little more difficult."

Albright shrugged. "Yeah, have to stay away from the press. You know, Fillmore's a great man. He could do wonders. His ideas aren't as radical as Blackman wants to make them sound."

Louongo offered insight from his murky place in the political universe. "Blackman's a vicious asshole who'll screw the entire country if given half a goddamn chance. Fillmore's a good sonofabitch. No contest."

Nathan and Max nodded. Case closed.

OK Journal

My View—Tommy Jacks

Perhaps Henry Blackman spends his off hours nursing crippled puppies. Maybe he donates every dollar he can spare to the least fortunate. Maybe he's just a teddy bear once you get to know him.

And maybe Howard Fillmore lives in anxious hope that no one will pick up some faint, almost invisible thread of evidence leading to a bulging bagful of secrets so abhorrent, even the most debased would cringe before them.

But here's what we have so far:

Fillmore has been open and honest, and not one person—count 'em: none—has offered any information that he is anything but a considerate and deliberate thinker with a political vision so democratic some think it's ide-alistic. Yes, he comes down on a side of some polarizing matters that runs against the predominant political grain in this state. But he's willing to talk.

Don't take my word for that. Find out for yourself. Invite Howard Fillmore to talk. He'll come, and he won't just give a speech. He'll discuss any political issue you care to bring up. And he'll *listen*. That's an observation, not merely an opinion.

He's willing to address matters that aren't comfortable for him. He knows he's starting from the back of the field as far as getting into the Senate is concerned. He knows Blackman has the pole position.

Blackman's record in this matter so far has been, let's say, "different." At least two experiences with press coverage have ended badly.

More than that, given the opportunity to demonstrate the kind of openness everyone should expect of someone who would be a U.S. Senator, Blackman has, to put it briefly, not done that. After the tank farm owned by his oil company erupted in flames of biblical proportion, he blamed an environmental group for setting it off. He said the group wants to tear down America.

We won't repeat the name given to the group because after weeks of contacting every source and combing through every file we can think to look up, we have found no evidence it exists.

That is not to accuse Blackman of lying. He could be duped. Tulsa police and fire departments only go on the information he's given them because they have to. After all, what if actual and insane people are behind the fire, and the authorities just blew off what Blackman gave them?

But don't try to discuss any of that with Blackman. You won't even hear "no comment," or "it's under investigation, so . . .," and certainly not, "Let's consider the possibilities." Instead, you'll get an X-rated blessing-out of anyone with enough gall to ask questions everyone wants answers for.

That's the difference in how these men present themselves.

16
HEAVEN AND HELL

In a surprise announcement, the Reverend Robert S. Olsen, famous faith healer and televangelist from Tulsa, entered the race for the U.S. Senate as an independent candidate. The move caught political observers off guard. It did not shock Olsen's followers, who had heard the renowned minister on many occasions say it was time for God's people to step into the ugly world of politics to save the country.

Olsen made his announcement standing outside his towering church. "It is with great humility that today I'm announcing my candidacy for the U.S. Senate seat from this great state of Oklahoma. All the proper paperwork, including a petition with almost twice the required signatures, has been filed with the Secretary of State. That paperwork says I'm running as an independent, but as my followers know, and as I want all of you to know, I'm running as a member of God's Party. Some say preachers don't belong in the dirty business of politics. Well, I say to them they're wrong. Who better than preachers to set this country straight, to correct the immoral paths so many of our fellow citizens are on today? I'm running to be a legislator, but also I'm running to be your beacon of truth, your hope for the future, your guide to a more prosperous and happier life.

Together we will change this country and bring God back to the United States Senate."

Amen.

Blackman was in his boat-sized Lincoln, alone, headed to Wichita. He had called Byron Cook to ask for a meeting. Henry sensed reluctance. Still, he fully understood the tension between them, if for no other reason than they knew a lot about each other.

The drive took about three hours, which gave Henry time to think. And being away from phones was good for his temperament. He wondered about Ed—didn't really care, just wondered. He hadn't seen him since their binge the other night. He knew he'd show up. But Ed being unavailable and unaccounted for nagged at him.

He thought about the preacher Olsen getting into the race. He'd met the loudmouth and was genuinely shocked by his gaudiness. The man reeked of cologne. He wore more jewelry than a harlot. He'd be a factor in the race, that was for sure. One of the common threads in most Oklahomans' lives was religion. But the term for a senator was six years. That was a long time to listen to Olsen in his sing-song voice telling you how bad you were. But Henry was unsure how to attack him without risk. He'd think of something. Maybe he liked girls—or even better, boys. He chuckled. He needed Ed to start doing some research.

Cook Oil and Gas was headquartered in a modest office building on the outskirts of downtown Wichita. Henry felt superior just looking at the nondescript, bland place. He remembered Cook as a plain man. And, he reminded himself, he also was ruthless.

"It's been a while, Henry. Looks like we've both aged a bit."

"Yeah, it's been some time." Henry eyed Byron. It was odd, but he still liked the guy. "When you're young, old farts tell you life is short, and you think they're full of shit. But now we know."

"Well, well. Henry Blackman, philosopher. Don't think I'd have guessed that." They chuckled. Maybe not in a good way, they connected. "What's on your mind?"

"I've screwed up pretty bad. Seems like it's my style to push until something breaks. Spent tons of money drilling where the wiseass geologists told me not to, and found nothing. Lost it all. So I'm cash-poor, but I've still got great assets. I'm going to sell Connex, and I think you should buy it." They conducted business the same way—no bullshit, get right to the point.

Still, it meant hours of going over details. Henry felt surprised by how much Cook knew. He could identify the good fields Connex controlled as well as he could.

"I'm on the ropes," Henry admitted, "and I've been honest with you. You can try and squeeze me and I'll walk away, file bankruptcy. If you want to get Connex at a fair price with a small 'I fucked up' discount, I think we can make a quick deal. And I can put all that fire bullshit behind me and go on and win the Senate seat. Think about that and how it could benefit you and your company. The other option looks like a senator who's by all accounts a communist, or maybe some religious nut with no regard for what businessmen need. I think there's a lot here that helps you—and of course, me, too."

Byron Cook nodded. "I think we can close this deal in sixty days." He extended his hand. Blackman took it and smiled.

"I was just in the coffee shop downstairs watching the news. Looks like Cook Oil and Gas is going to buy Connex. What do you think that does for Blackman?" Vince had just walked into the press room.

"Wow. I'm surprised some other company would jump into the Connex mess. Who's Cook Oil and Gas?" Tommy looked up from working on a column.

"Owned lock, stock, and barrel by Byron Cook, the guy who started the Freedom Branch Society. His goal is to take the country as far right as it can go without having a dictator. Then again, he might think a dictator would be just fine. He's very pro-business and anti-government. I think the timing of this deal has to do with the Connex stock offering having to be pulled. The business editor told me he thought Connex was out of cash and if something didn't happen, they'd have to file bankruptcy. Of course, that's the same guy who told me to sell all my McDonald's stock—financial genius, he's not."

"Hmm. Blackman will say he sold his business so he can spend his time running for Senate. The fire and the stupid EDL lie will be forgotten, and he'll be some people's ideal candidate—a rich former businessman who can get things done." Tommy started to worry.

Vince shrugged. "Going to make our lives a lot more fun, though. Now we'll have a general election between a far-right, overbearing rich ex-businessman, a liberal intellectual college president, and a pompous theocratic TV preacher. We couldn't have paid for better entertainment."

Tommy wasn't laughing. "Let's just hope nobody gets killed."

Albright knew when he asked for a ride that Louongo had no idea he meant taking him all the way to Enid. Having Louongo drive out of his city habitat would make him nervous and irritable—not the perfect road-trip companion.

"You sure this guy should be hiring you to run his campaign?" Sure enough, Louongo sounded annoyed.

"Hell no, he shouldn't be hiring me. He should hire someone who lives in this state and is connected with the media and is not a magnet for controversy. Right off, though, it makes you admire the poor fool." Albright knew he should tell Fillmore the idea wasn't a good one, but he couldn't help it. He wanted to be involved. "The only reason he thinks he wants me involved is Bill Anderson. He needs Bill's endorsement. So Bill says to him, 'You need the guy who guided my campaign to failure.' Fillmore thinks that's stupid but can't bring himself to say so. So, here we are in this cramped car headed to Enid. No logic at all."

"My people tell me this three-person race means nobody knows what'll happen. Even that whacko preacher could win." Louongo's "people" had a much better handle on criminal matters than political ones, but the two overlapped, and their opinions had a ring of truth.

Albright's real goals were to be on the inside of the campaign and to write a book about the experience. The preacher joining in was an amazing gift to the dynamics of the story. He had given thought to being the campaign manager but knew that would be a serious mistake. While he appreciated his old friend Anderson's blind faith in him, it wasn't something he'd let a friend do. Fillmore had a small chance because he was a good man who believed in the people and would fight for them. But he'd need every advantage he could get. Hanging Albright and his messy past around his neck was not an advantage.

Still, Albright was traveling to Enid to interview for the manager's job. It was all prearranged by Anderson, and Albright was tempted by the attractive challenge. But as they drove, he made up his mind. He would offer his services as an anonymous consultant and recommend Fillmore hire Mary Ann Peterson, whom he'd met during his work with Anderson's campaign. Mary Ann had her own PR firm, was one-hundred percent Oklahoman, and knew what she was doing. A female campaign manager would raise eyebrows, but it was perfect for Fillmore. And she was well connected with the media throughout the state.

"Hey, this is a nice-looking school. How the hell did it end up here?" Louongo seemed impressed with the manicured campus but chose to wait in the car while Albright was meeting in the administration building. He had no idea where Louongo earned his law degree but noted that his attitude about the administration building suggested a traumatic past in a place much like it.

"Bill Anderson highly recommends you to manage my campaign," Fillmore said. "He says he thinks you're a genius when it comes to politics."

"Probably should give back those compromising photos I

have of him; you think?"

Fillmore laughed out loud. "Well, yeah, he should be let off the hook. Do you even want to be the campaign manager?"

"I'd love to. But I don't hate you, so I think it'd be a mistake. Let me tell you what I think should happen." Albright laid out his plan, and gave his recommendation for Mary Ann Peterson, who Fillmore knew from some dealings with her related to the college.

Fillmore was clearly impressed. "I see why Bill trusts you. I agree completely. She sounds like she will be perfect. I'll approach her today, and if she says yes, I'll have her call you. Agreed?"

"Agreed." *Let the fun begin.*

My View—Tommy Jacks

Now it gets interesting. Henry Blackman's problems with Connex—the biblical-scale tank farm fire, its effect on a planned public stock offering, and the evidently nonexistent "environmentalist" group Blackman blamed for setting it—could be over, just like that.

In simple terms, Blackman's going to sidestep and soft-shoe out of the Connex spotlight.

It's a smart move for him, especially since the doggone downright Rev. Robert S. Olsen decided it was high time to see if he should take the independent road from the exalted pulpit of his massive church in Tulsa to the bully pulpit of the U.S. Senate.

Between him, the Republican Blackman and Democrat Howard Fillmore, that makes three frontrunners, which opens things up in ways we can only guess at.

For now, though, Blackman's pulled a big rabbit out of a tiny hat, just as time was about to run out. If his insistence that a phantom group of unhinged pyromaniacs set off the tank farm fire didn't pan out *and* he wound up being compelled by law to pull the plug on his plans for a public stock offering, his candidacy might have found itself in big trouble in little time.

Worse, we'd be bound by journalistic duty to ask questions with real knuckles on them, like, "Why, Mr. Blackman, should the people of Oklahoma consider you a good candidate for the Senate after this flagrant fiasco concerning your business? And why do you seem to be the only person on earth familiar with the group you said started the tank farm fire?"

I mean, look what happened the last time anyone asked him a question that wasn't half as tough as either of those. Such *language*. And on TV, no less.

It's a cinch we won't have to worry about that with Olsen. He'll bring up the name of the Almighty, all righty, but never in vain. And the man has a state-wide reach that, to be honest, no one else has. Just turn on the television set on Sunday morning, and he's there, on time and paid for, for a whole hour—or maybe it only seems that long. His sermon last week timed out at 25 minutes and 38 seconds, for the sake of thorough reporting, but that includes four long moments of pause while the sea of faithful—thousands, it appeared—roared.

It does raise the question of why someone with that much of a positive thing going for him would put any of it on the line for the sake of seamy, hardball politics.

Perhaps we should put that one to the Rev. Olsen. We wouldn't hesitate. Because, praise the Lord, at least he won't blister our ears just for asking. ❧

17
CRIMES AND PUNISHMENT

Ed Black had been laid up in a bed in the small hospital in Bixby for what seemed like a couple of years. It was actually only a few days. He still ached all over, but he was ready to leave. Connex was paying for it, and he should have just relaxed and enjoyed his time away from that asshole Blackman. He'd left the blowhard at the Mayo. Years ago, there used to be a great whorehouse just north of Bixby, and he'd been drunk enough for the idea to find the place to make sense.

He never found the whorehouse, but he did find a roadside bar where he quickly pissed off about half its male clientele. Two of the biggest were elected to beat the crap out of him. They might have finished him off, but they got thirsty and went back inside. That gave the bartender time to call Bixby Police, who took Ed to the hospital. They didn't arrest or charge him but advised him that once released from the hospital, he'd best leave town. Ed agreed.

But he'd do it his way. Ed resisted everything and everyone who disagreed with him—even some who didn't. He started out in the oil fields doing whatever he wanted and screw the world. He rubbed everyone the wrong way. Henry was a bit smoother with people, mainly because everyone who looked into his cold eyes feared him. Soon, under Henry's guidance, they became a dangerous, if odd, team.

Now Ed had money and even a little prestige. And he hated Henry. He knew that without him, he'd have been nothing and probably long dead. But he still hated him. He knew he was bad, *but Henry was evil.* All Henry's success came at a price paid by whoever was in the way, exacted by Ed. That didn't conflict with Ed's sense of right or wrong. It was just that Henry always seemed to be above it all. He treated Ed worse than anyone he knew until he needed him to carry out some mayhem. Then he was his pal again.

Ed knew he was done with Henry. He wouldn't be treated like scum anymore.

"Good morning, Mister Black." The doctor just seemed to appear out of nowhere. "X-rays and lab tests tell us you may have suffered some internal injuries. Like to send you to a hospital in Tulsa where they can find out more. We'll take you by ambulance. Ready?" The doctor had been offered bribes to discharge the man in Room 105. The nursing staff hated Ed, and several threatened to quit if he stayed a minute longer.

"Hell, no. No way in hell am I going to another hospital in a damn ambulance. I'm leaving now." Ed began removing various attachments.

The doctor moved quickly to try and stop him. "Mister Black, you might die."

"Fuck that. Die?" Ed laughed. "I've been goin' to die since the day I was born." Ed put on his clothes. The doctor retreated while he scribbled notes on his clipboard. Ed discharged himself and had walked outside before he realized his car was still at the bar. He went back inside and described the bar to the receptionist at the front desk. She frowned while admitting she knew the place, about three miles down the road. She pointed in the direction. He headed that way on foot.

"Press room. Jacks." Tommy seemed to be the only one who ever answered the press room phone. Of course, it was usually for him.

"Tommy, could you come see the governor right now?"

"Sure, Gail. I'll be right there." He hoped it had to do with the fight at the Corporation Commission.

"Tommy, do you know Walter Jefferson, in charge of the Corporation Commission?" The governor gestured toward Jefferson as he got up to shake hands. "I think this still needs to be off the record, but we're getting close to going public. Is that okay?" The governor paused.

"I guess so, sir. But I can't sit on it for long."

"Let me think about where we are after this conversation. Walter, tell Tommy what you just told me." The governor nodded toward Jefferson.

"When Mister Young brought us copies of inspector reports and asked us to comment on them, we discovered those reports weren't in our files. Will Lyles, head of the oil and gas division, was shocked. They appeared to be legit, although we said they weren't. Lyles confronted Tim Hudson, the clerk responsible for those files. Hudson insisted to Lyles they were forgeries. Lyles didn't believe him and told Hudson he personally would look at all inspectors' reports involving Connex. Hudson started yelling he wouldn't stand for anyone calling him a liar. The office staff overheard and called the capitol police. By then, Lyles tried to push past Hudson, and Hudson hit him, breaking his nose. Hudson started to leave when the capitol police showed up, and they decided they needed to report it to Oklahoma City PD. So they held Hudson while Lyles was taken to the clinic and then to a hospital. Oklahoma City police came, arrested Hudson and took him downtown. At that point I was informed and went to the hospital. I talked to Lyles and decided that since we were uncertain what happened with the files, we shouldn't press charges. But like I just told the governor, I was mostly worried about bad publicity." He took a deep breath. "Since that time, we've reviewed our files and discovered that all inspection reports for Connex are missing. We think Hudson removed them, and maybe he was paid to. I've contacted Oklahoma City police and have advised them we've decided to press charges. We've also contacted State Police and advised them we believe Hudson destroyed or stole official state reports, which is a felony."

"Is there any way to recover those files?" Tommy felt sorry for Jefferson. Judging by his body language, this wouldn't be good for his career.

Jefferson kind of slumped. "None. These reports are routine, and not considered secret or critical. We don't micro-film them or anything. If they've been destroyed, they're gone."

"Tommy, you said you thought this could have to do with the Connex fire, and we now agree. But we have nothing to tell us why Hudson might've taken or destroyed the records. All we know for sure is they're gone and Hudson's disappeared." The governor looked unhappy, conflicted about what to say or do next. "We shouldn't keep this out of the paper. We had an employee who may have committed a serious crime. We should've been more candid with Vince. Lyles and Jefferson both tried to do what they thought best at the time. If there's a consequence, we'll deal with it. All we ask is that you give a fair account of what happened and not use our candor and speculation with you against us. We'll pursue all appropriate action to determine what did happen and bring anyone involved in this to justice. You should also know that Jefferson submitted his resignation to me, and I have not accepted it. He and Lyles will need to clean this mess up and come up with procedures so this can't happen again."

Tommy left. There was always a lot of talk about the character and ethics of politicians; either they had them or not. Bud Evans demonstrated both.

Back in the press room, Tommy called Vince at *Journal* headquarters. "Got a good lead for you. Governor Evans said you were right and they misled you to cover their behinds, but we should be nice when we report that little tidbit."

"What the hell are you talking about?"

"Crimes."

OK Journal

My View—Tommy Jacks

It looks like I spoke too soon. I hate when that happens.

Don't get mad. Let me explain.

A few days ago, a fistfight broke out in the offices of the Corporation Commission. It had to do with missing records, which might have had to do with a dead oil and gas inspector and, in an interesting twist, the same company being sold by Henry Blackman, a Republican candidate for next year's U.S. Senate race.

And it traces back further to a guy named Buck Howard, an inspector who worked for the commission and who kept getting run off Connex's tank farms, even if he shouldn't have been. Howard was supposed to file paperwork after each visit because that was his job, by law. But sometimes he had to sneak in to get a few readings for inspection forms.

We suspect he may have known something was up. Howard began keeping his paperwork, or copies of it, and sharing them with a reporter for the *Tulsa Herald*, Matt Tomas. Tomas made sure he wasn't the only one who had them, partly by sharing with a fellow reporter at the *Herald*. That was a good thing because Tomas went underground only a few days later and only recently came back up for air, with a lot of questions to answer. The other *Herald* reporter shared the documents with the *Journal*.

But Howard was found dead weeks ago on the banks of the Arkansas River just outside Connex's tank farm, which is only beginning to recover from an apocalypse-scale fire set there. Blackman insists it was ignited by some environmental group that we'll just have to agree never existed.

Also not found were the inspection reports on Connex's tank farms that Howard filed, or should have filed, at the Corporation Commission up to the time he decided to start keeping them to himself.

That's what the fistfight was about.

Will Lyles, the head of the commission's oil and gas division, saw the files Howard left with the *Herald*. He admits he suspected they were genuine, and that what they said made him anxious. So, he went into the bowels of the division's office to ask after earlier reports.

The clerk in charge, a Tim Hudson, raised a fuss that became an argument ending with a right cross to Lyles's nose. Lyles went to the hospital, and Hudson to the back of an Oklahoma City Police cruiser. But Walter Jefferson, chairman of the commission, decided at the time not to press charges. He wanted to get deeper into the matter and talk to Hudson.

But Hudson vanished.

So, let's review. One man is dead. One is missing. Another went missing but turned up again. And who knows how many reports about the safety and ecological impact of a Connex oil tank farm are gone—probably for good, Jefferson fears. The tank farm is a total loss, and Blackman just closed a deal to sell it along with his company.

Maybe Henry Blackman still has a lot of questions to answer. And he should watch his language when he does. No amount of expletives is going to clear this mess away. 🐛

18
VOTE IF YOU MUST

Primary election brought two bands of violent storms with torrential rains moving through Oklahoma City in one day, and caused major disruptions. Neighborhoods went without power, and traffic became nightmarish. News coverage concentrated on the lethal weather and all but ignored the voting. By late afternoon, turnout was at a record low.

Some thought that might mean surprises. Most still expected the outcome would be wins for the favorites. Henry Blackman for the Republicans and Howard Fillmore for the Democrats. Robert S. Olsen, an independent, didn't appear on the ballots. Dense, dark clouds turned afternoon into night. Watch parties were canceled. Flooded streets hit Oklahoma City especially hard, and more rounds of storms were predicted through the evening, making the day a record-setter.

Each major candidate put out statements asking voters to be careful heading to the polls, to pay attention to weather alerts and seek safety as needed. Olsen added a declaration that seemed to suggest his followers would be okay not only because they could stay home, but also because God was watching over them; the subtle implication being that God didn't have the same concern for his opponents' voters.

Ray Jacks pushed the intercom button. "Yes."

"There is a Joe Louongo at the front entrance, says he wants to see you."

"Sure, send him up."

Louongo never just showed up. Ray wondered what he might want. The investigative group had authority to hire him to assist in their dealings, but so far, they had not used him much. Maybe that was it—he needed business.

"Mister Louongo. What are you doing out in this weather?"

"My whole fuckin' life's a storm. What the hell do I care about a little rain?" Louongo took a seat. "My newest client asked me to see you."

"Who's that?" Most of Louongo's clients were people Ray Jacks would prefer nothing to do with or even for them to know his name.

"Loretta Lynch."

Ray reacted with surprise. "What's happened?" It was a genuine shock that pious Loretta would even know about Louongo, much less ask him to represent her.

"She was arrested for the murder of T.D. McFadden, your old boss. Seems somewhere along the way, she knew you knew me, and had my number." He frowned. "Not real sure she was ready to meet me. I think I embarrassed her a couple of times. Shit, I didn't know she was some kind of church lady. Why the fuck would somebody call *me* if language offended 'em?"

Good point. Ray had to chuckle while he thought about ultra-religious Loretta meeting Louongo for the first time. "Is she still in jail?"

"Yeah. Doesn't have the money to post bond. So, she'll stay put until the first hearing next week. Could be best for her. She's not a flight risk. But after the cops interviewed her, they put her on suicide watch. She's in a private cell, and they check on her about every half hour."

"Why do they think she killed T.D.?"

"A neighbor saw her leaving about the time McFadden was shot. He didn't know her; all he gave the cops was a description. Well, as they're investigating, they interviewed her because she was his office manager and thought she matched the description. They did a lineup, and the guy picked her out. About then she called me. Today the cops searched her house and found a gun. They're saying it's a match."

"They've run tests?"

"No. But it's the same caliber, and it was fired in the last few months. I guess they'll find more. But as it stands right now, the eyewitness putting her at the crime scene and the gun was enough to charge her."

"She's the nicest, kindest person on this planet. Why would she do that?"

"Beats the hell out of me. She's not my typical client. She was so polite, I felt like I was visiting my mother, although my mother wasn't *that* polite. I got her to sign a rep agreement, but she didn't ask me much and didn't tell me anything. She was mostly worried about her house and her pets. Ray, I'm not sure I'm the right person to help this lady."

Ray thought, *my goodness, the mean-ass Louongo has a heart. Who would've thought?* "Let me try to see her. I guess anything's possible, but Loretta shooting T.D. doesn't fit."

Much of the state was under either a severe storm warning or a tornado watch. Experienced weather people said they didn't remember a day like it. Flooding in Tulsa and Oklahoma City turned serious. The governor declared an emergency and sent National Guard troops to help. Voting slowed to a trickle. Some polling places closed under threat of floods.

Reverend Olsen's campaign, although it wasn't involved in the primaries, demanded that the governor and state election officials keep polls open through the next day. The governor's office replied it didn't have authority to do that. The Oklahoma State Election Board issued a statement that basically said they didn't believe they could do that, but it sounded like a good idea and they would get back to everyone on it.

The polls closed. The election board tallied the results. There would be no extra day. The results were as predicted.

The next beautiful, sunny morning, Mathew Tomas met Louongo in front of the First National Bank building where the local FBI office was. He carried a package, handling it like he was afraid it might explode.

"Ready to spill your guts?"

"You're sure this will work?" Tomas found Louongo quite odd at times, and now he had to trust him.

"Hell, yes. I already told you. They agreed; no charges. The state doesn't give a shit, either. The FBI just wants everything you know about your cousin. Give them that package, and all is forgiven."

"What if they change their minds?"

"My god, do you not trust anybody? Sonofabitch, it's the fuckin' FBI. They can't just tell you one thing and do another. Where would this country be if they did shit like that?"

"Okay. I guess it'll be all right."

"Sure, it'll be fine."

They took the elevator, and Louongo spoke to the lady behind the glass barrier. An agent came out and escorted them into a conference room. Tomas carried in his package.

A very distinguished-looking man entered.

"Mister Tomas, glad to meet you. My name is Paul Swartz. I'm out of the D.C. office. I was involved in the investigation of matters to which Chuck Branson was connected. When I heard your story, I thought it best if I met with you. I assume the package is the one you kept."

"Yeah." Tomas seemed a little intimidated by Swartz. He slid the package toward him.

"Let me take this out to be examined before we open it." Swartz took the package out and returned to address Matt. "I know some of the story, but maybe it would be best if you told me everything that happened between you and your cousin."

"Sure." Tomas covered everything, including the meeting he was supposed to have had with Tommy at the Skirvin before he saw Chuck and panicked. To his ear it sounded rehearsed. He hoped Swartz believed him.

"Do you have any idea where your cousin is now?"

"No. He's pretty good at disappearing."

"Do you think he'd harm you?"

Matt nodded. "If he thought I did anything against him, he wouldn't rest until he got revenge. He was always like that. I don't know what's in the package, but if it's something he wants and I don't have it, he'll kill me. Do you know where he is?"

"No. We tracked him for a while. Now we don't know where he is. We were surprised when we found out you'd seen him here. It was the last place we thought he'd show up. We can arrange protection for you and your family. You should know it won't be all the time, or forever. You may want to consider moving or changing your identity. We can help with that."

"I don't know about that. I have my job and my career. Things were just starting to click for me at the paper. Changing my name means losing everything. Maybe if it's just a little money or a small amount of drugs, he won't bother me again."

They heard a knock on the door. Swartz got up and opened the door slightly to talk in whispers to someone and came back. "Looks like we have a bigger problem than we thought. There were several thousand dollars in cash in the package, and certificates of deposit, payable to the bearer, from a bank in the Cayman Islands. The total value is right at one million dollars."

Tomas turned pale.

"What the fuck, a million bucks. Shit. He'll sure as hell be back for that kind of dough." Louongo was very insightful when it came to criminal behavior.

OK Journal

My View—Tommy Jacks

Let's hear it for Bruce Irving, Nick Hightower, Frank Clayton, Sam Elliott and Oliver Howser:

Thanks for showing up, guys. Have a nice life.

Irving and Hightower opposed Howard Fillmore in the Democratic primary for the upcoming election to the U.S. Senate seat that Rick Butler can hardly wait to bail out of. We can't say much about either because it seemed like they never had much to say for themselves. As far as could be determined, their common campaign slogan was, "I'm a farmer. Or a rancher. Sort of. Maybe. Don't ask."

Irving said he worked for or with or maybe somewhere near the state Peanut Commission, but it's hard to tell because the phone there seems to be disconnected—maybe ripped out of the wall. Hightower mentioned something about being a deputy sheriff in Osage County, but no one there seems interested in tracking that down. Perhaps as a result, a lot of other farmers and ranchers in this state carried just as many precincts as they did together, which was none.

Fillmore pursued a different strategy, which seemed to work. He takes the banner for the political party with a donkey for a mascot, in a walk.

Clayton and Elliott at least had traceable political pedigrees. Clayton came fresh off two terms on the Oklahoma City council—and oh, the battles he fought there—while Elliott was once a Tulsa County commissioner. Their collective reticence on the campaign trail is a trifle more puzzling. Why didn't they go after such a vulnerable frontrunner as Henry Blackman, hammer and tongs?

The man was practically obscured by swarming rumors about his company and the doomsday-scale fire that leveled his oil tank farm in Tulsa. Questions about possible connections to the ultra-right and frankly frightening Freedom Branch Society still hang out here. And let's not forget what happens to his language anytime he hears a direct question. But, there Blackman goes, straight to Election Day in November.

And Oliver Howser's misfortune was to file as an unspecified independent. The rock-ribbed right Rev. Robert S. Olsen of Tulsa would likely have won a primary for independents. Howser, whose greatest campaign moment came and went with the announcement of his intention to abolish the United Nations—which no senator can do—threw in the towel the day after the primaries, without a vote cast.

Maybe he, like the king of Babylon, saw the writing on the wall in the wrath of the Almighty. That seemed somehow to come into play on the behalf of Olsen, bringing forth the whirlwind and the greatest floods since Noah. Olsen didn't claim credit, but he did say his voters likely could walk on water all the way to the polls, had they found the need to, all the way to November.

Amen. Go figure, and tremble.

And then there's sad news about a sad fate. Oklahoma City police have made an arrest in the death of T.D. McFadden, once a Democratic state representative out of Oklahoma County. McFadden's fall from grace and favor were great. He fell so far that hardly anyone raised an eyebrow when his body was found months ago. Sadder still is that the suspect is a trusted former employee of his, who no one would have thought capable of such a thing. We're watching and hoping for the best, and preparing for the worst, which is pretty close to how things tend to wind up.

19

WORK HARD AND PROSPER

"You'd better understand, Tommy Jacks—if you keep treating me like an afterthought, I will dump you like a hot potato." Patsy sat in the car with her arms crossed, ready to scream or cry or both.

"Look, I'm sorry. How can I say it any other way? No excuses—*I'm sorry.* I got caught up in stuff. Please don't be so mad at me, okay?" He couldn't believe he'd ignored Patsy to chase a story or an interview. That and his schedule on *Oklahoma AM* had him running all day long. And he knew it had to stop.

"I know you think all this is very important—which I guess it is. But if you can't get your priorities right, you'll end up just like your dad used to be. How'd that feel when you were a kid? Do you want to be like that?"

That hurt because it was true. He knew the pain of benign neglect. Now he was doing it to the person he cared the most about, all because he had to handle something important, or at least what he thought was important. And he'd always told himself he'd never do that.

They were headed to his parents' house for dinner, which wasn't sounding like a good idea anymore. Patsy was mad and he was sure she'd talked to Tracy, who would be mad, too, which meant his dad would be mad.

"No. Of course I don't. I messed up. I'll do better." He was losing energy. "Look—let's stop at Risso's. Have a beer. I'll call Tracy and just tell her we need to talk and we'll be over in a few days. I don't want to deal with everyone being mad at me."

Patsy looked at him. "Okay. I'll call and tell her it was my idea for us to talk it over. If you call her, she'll get mad because she fixed dinner."

"Right." Tommy was realizing that being close to people was hard and took work. He hoped he could pull it off.

"Tommy! Patsy! What a wonderful surprise." Larry Lopez, the owner of Risso's, was one of their favorite people.

"Hey, Larry. Great to see you. Think we're just going to have a beer and maybe a pizza later. We're going into the bar."

"Of course, of course. How're your dad and Tracy doing? Guess they're big shots now, eh?" Larry smiled.

Taylor Albright was number one in the world of Oklahoma City gossip before he left town, followed by Joe Louongo and Larry Lopez at number three. They were a veritable library of unsourced, unproven and mostly untrue information. But within their gossip lay vital facts.

"Doing well. What's the story on the election, Larry? Who's going to win?"

"Don't spread this around." He was talking to a reporter and columnist for a daily newspaper, so of course he couldn't have cared less if he used it. "My gut says the good Reverend Robert S. Olsen wins in a tight race, the first elected senator of the God Party."

Tommy was stunned. Larry always seemed to be so connected. That seemed off the wall. "Any chance you're a supporter of the reverend?"

"Me? You've got to be kiddin'. That man wants a society run by his biblical laws. Poor old Risso's would be closed by the Bible-carrying moral police the first week he took power. My vote's going to Fillmore. But I'm tellin' you what's being said. And if you look at the numbers in a three-person race where both the major party candidates have big problems, the preacher wins."

Tommy still grappled with the idea. He felt a tug on his arm. "Sorry." He escorted Patsy to a back booth to settle in with beers and pretzels.

She smiled. He felt relieved. She took his hand. "You really love that stuff, don't you?"

"Political gossip?" he asked. She nodded. "Yeah. Guess so. It's like those soap operas. The stories never end, just different actors coming and going. I know," he shrugged, "I get too involved. But I'm determined to do better. Even take some time off. How about that?"

She knew he was trying to make her happy, and that this was who he was and she should not try to change him. If she couldn't live with it, she should just leave and not hound him into misery. "I love you, Tommy."

"I love you, too." He wasn't sure what was going on. She seemed to act differently from a few minutes ago.

"I'm going to call Tracy and tell her we'll be over Friday. Okay?"

"Sure. We'll bring dinner. Burgers and fries from Johnnie's."

Chuck Branson ordered his second margarita at the massive bar of The Kentucky Club in Ciudad Juarez. The Kentucky was famous for inventing the margarita. Chuck thought it was the best damned drink in the world. He knew he wasn't completely safe from the FBI in Mexico. Still, it felt safer being on the wrong side of the Rio Grande.

But he had to get that package back from his stupid cousin. He knew Matt wouldn't open it because he was scared of everything, especially him. Chuck only sent it because he wanted to keep it away from the feds until he could decide what to do with it. But then that idiot Matt went underground. He considered kidnapping his wife, but also considered the chance he'd already given it to the feds. If he did that, it crossed the line. Chuck had to kill him.

Chuck was just a small fry. He and a buddy started smuggling drugs in the Air Force, an arrangement that fell apart with consequences tragic for his friend. And in a strange twist of fate Chuck wound up as the police beat reporter for the *OK Journal,* which meant going more or less straight for a while. But after Oklahoma City's top crime boss decided things were getting too hot and hightailed it out of the country, Chuck saw an opportunity. He started working with new guys who turned out to be stupid amateurs. They screwed up everything in a hurry. He looked for a way to cash out. He had the name of the brains behind the previous boss, Doctor Ralph Jenkins. He hadn't planned on doing anything with that but figured it might give him leverage if the FBI started after him. He figured he could trade that name for a lighter sentence; maybe even get off scot-free.

He felt pretty cocky until he heard the Jenkins guy had been shot by a senator at a mansion in Nichols Hills. Suddenly his idea had no value. He'd followed the doctor before, just to see where he lived. When he heard he'd been killed, he went to the doctor's house and broke in. He found packed luggage and a package in the entryway. No doubt the good doctor had also planned on getting out of town. He heard sirens, grabbed the package and left.

Even after he opened it he wasn't sure what he had, aside from the cash. The certificates of deposit didn't make sense to him. And how would he get to Cayman where you would have to go to cash them in, wherever the hell that was? It all made him nervous. He knew the FBI had him on their radar—they'd followed him a couple of times and were tough to lose. If they caught him with this stuff, he'd spend a long time in prison. He took a few hundred from the cash, repackaged the rest and sent it to Matt. Once things cooled down, he would get it back and figure it out. Chuck tried to call Matt, who was always out working, but before he could get in touch the FBI got on his tail again. He managed once more to lose them and headed south fast.

After he learned Matt would be at a symposium in Oklahoma City, he decided to risk going there to make contact. But before he could, he spotted Tommy Jacks. The idea turned risky in a hotel full of reporters, especially ones who knew him. He headed back to Texas and crossed into Mexico. Chuck knew returning to Oklahoma was risky, but he had no choice. He'd either get his money back or kill Matt or both. If it came to it, he'd die trying.

Two bus lines catered to Mexican customers who regularly scheduled rides to San Antonio, Austin, Dallas, and Oklahoma City, but not Tulsa. It promised to be a long and painful trip. But he swore it would be the last lousy cheap bus ride he would take.

OK Journal

My View—Tommy Jacks

Consideration of the upcoming election for U.S. Senate, now only three months away, is best approached after a few (all right, several) draughts of above-the-limit beer, some nearly authentic Italian pizza and some existential and diverting comfort.

Only then can we handle prophecy of biblical proportion. A gravely delivered prediction from a familiar and frequently prophetic source says the hard-right Rev. Robert S. Olsen's walk-on-water show is no fluke. Oliver Howser saw the same and abandoned ship.

A lot of politically minded people, most especially the veteran ward heelers in every corner of this state are edging close to panic.

Henry Blackman, the winning Republican candidate, and Howard Fillmore, the Democratic victor, each had two opponents in their primaries, but they dissolved in the rain. Meanwhile, Olsen's faithful—and we mean faithful—kept their powder dry.

Now bar owners are pondering other lines of business, legal or otherwise. Newsstand operators wonder how to tell suppliers to leave the *Playboys* in the trucks. A whole state shakes in its boots at the idea of people actually having to act like the upright sorts they've always been proud to claim they are.

Indeed, God moves in a mysterious way.

20
POLITICS AND GRIEF

The general election season began. The first volley was delivered by the Blackman campaign in two television commercials for stations in the Oklahoma City and Tulsa markets. The first focused on Howard Fillmore. It showed a picture of a young Fillmore with hair combed in a duck-tail, and asked Oklahomans if they wanted an ultra-liberal greaser to represent their great state in the nation's capital. In contrast, Blackman's face appeared with a waving flag in the background, narrated by, "a proud American, Henry Blackman, your next U.S. Senator." Political experts deemed it effective because it established differences Blackman's campaign wanted to emphasize.

The other was about the Reverend Olsen, full of screen shots of him laying hands on people during his healing services. Everything, including the voice-over— "once again, Reverend Olsen offers healing rituals for money"—mocked him.

The backlash was immediate and furious. Even people who didn't support Olsen took offense. Blackman's campaign pulled the commercial, but the damage was done. He was labeled a religion-hater in a state full of religious people. His camp hastily fired the advertising agency, reputedly number one in the state, and hired a new one, reputedly the number-two firm. The second firm drafted a press release saying Blackman hadn't approved the commercial and it was the first ad agency's fault that it ran. The first agency reacted with a defamation lawsuit against Blackman, his campaign, and the second agency.

Olsen's campaign only officially replied, "No comment." It did release a statement that the reverend would step down from the ministry of his church, following legal advice.

Olsen was beset by reporters outside his church on the way to his limousine.

"Why are you quitting your church, reverend?"

"Does this have to do with the negative ad campaign against you by the Blackman camp?"

The reverend paused to gaze at the gathered news people, whom he could have avoided if he'd used the rear exit. "This has nothing to do with the shocking commercial run by Henry Blackman, who apparently thinks it's appropriate to make fun of people's religious beliefs. I'm stepping down from my ministry with a heavy heart because I've been told by my legal advisors that there could be a conflict with certain aspects of IRS regulations. It was a complete surprise to me that America, the greatest country on this good earth, would have rules preventing a religious person from running for elected office. If elected, I will look into this travesty and get it repealed. For now, I will turn the church over to my loyal assistant minister. I'll work every hour of every day to win this race for the people of Oklahoma, and for God."

"Press room. Jacks."

"Dick Fitzgerald called. Said the Tulsa police chief just held a news conference and said the coroner's report was complete on Buck Howard." Vince sounded a little winded.

"Jeez, about time."

"Yeah. Never said what the holdup was. But he said it was definitely murder. They believe Howard was killed up by the tanks and tossed down the riverbank. Blow to the head, probably with something heavy and sharp, based on impressions in the skull. They have no suspects, and the investigations is at a standstill. How about that for great police work?"

"Nothing about questioning Connex's security?"

"Nothing. Dick said the news conference ended with the chief's assistants passing out a press release that more or less stated what he'd just said, and a copy of the coroner's report. Then they left."

"They can't be that stupid, can they? It has to be Blackman or some of his goons."

"Yeah, but thinking and knowing are two different things. I don't know enough about 'Sammy the Cop' to know if he's stupid or just being cautious. But I don't imagine you'd speculate on a crime being committed by a leading citizen unless you had a ton of proof."

"Guess not. Have you heard anything about Tomas?"

"Nope. I called the *Herald* and asked to speak to him, and they told me he was on a sabbatical. How the hell do you get a sabbatical at a newspaper? I'd like one." Vince was working at least two jobs at the *Journal* and it was starting to take a toll.

"Guess he's dealing with the legal mess because of Chuck, and maybe hiding, besides. I'm going to run by Louongo's and see if he'll tell me anything. We need to keep trying to talk to Tomas. Despite his problems, he's the best source we have about any of this."

"I agree. I'll try and contact his wife. But after that I think we're at a dead end with him unless he calls us."

Tommy went back to work on his column. He did not hear the person enter the press room.

"Well, well. You really *do* work."

Tommy jumped at Albright's voice. "Hey, yeah. Some days."

"Sorry I startled you. You know, I've been reading your stuff, even when I was in New York. You're gettin' better all the time. You may have a gift for this sort of thing." Albright grinned awkwardly. He never looked comfortable handing out compliments.

Tommy smiled. "Thanks. What's goin' on?"

"Wanted to get your insights on the reverend. I've got a good understanding of Blackman, but Olsen isn't something I've seen before. Is he for real or is that a show?"

"A bit of both. I think at his core he believes in his message and his God, but it's definitely wrapped up in a show-biz package. When he started, he ran a small con with his 'healing hands' routine, I think. And I bet Blackman's people got some of that dirt, which prompted them to make that commercial. But even if it was a con, it was a good one. The people he might've been fleecing then are now some of his biggest supporters. And running negative ads against him, his church, his followers, or his religion is like stomping through a minefield."

"Yeah, Blackman found that out." Albright was thoughtful. "Fillmore's already on the defensive. How do you think we can turn that around?"

"Am I a political consultant now?" Tommy grinned. Albright shrugged. "You'd have to give credit to the reverend for taking his moral beliefs to the public forum of a political race. Then you have to subtly wonder about an extremely religious person establishing policies for everyone. What does that mean for farm policies, taxes, roads, and schools—all those issues that have impact on people's everyday lives and pocketbooks? Be careful talking about that, though. With Blackman, you have to attack hard and often. Everything suspect about him—and that's a lot—has to be attacked. If Fillmore lets Blackman attack him without a hard, direct comeback, he'll be labeled a coward afraid to fight for his own skin. Blackman's a bully. The only way to deal with a bully is to fight back."

Albright nodded. "Do you really think Olsen could win?"

"It doesn't matter what I think. Larry, the owner of Risso's, says he can. It's people like Larry, and the ones he talks to, who decide. And, yes, they might vote for Olsen. If I was Fillmore, I'd be worried about the reverend."

Ray waited at the city jail where Louongo had arranged his meeting with Loretta Lynch. He felt nervous. He knew this would be emotional, and he had no answers for her. Besides, the last time he'd been there, he was a prisoner himself. All his instincts said to leave. He stayed.

Loretta entered with a shy smile. After the guard left, an awkward minute passed before anyone said anything.

"Are you okay, Loretta?"

"No. I'd say I'm very far from okay, Mister Jacks. I've committed a horrible sin. And I'm ready to pay my penance. But I'm not okay."

Ray had learned enough to know she likely had shot T.D., but it still felt like a shock to hear her admit it. "Why did you do it?"

"I just lost my mind." Loretta began to cry softly. "That job was the only thing holding me and my husband together. He had brain cancer. He was going through a real hard time with his chemotherapy." She paused. "When the business shut down, my insurance was canceled. I just couldn't believe it. They said I could continue the policy as an individual, but it would cost almost three times what we'd been paying, and I didn't have a job." Ray held her hand, saying nothing. "I looked at everything," she went on. "Tried to borrow from some of my relatives, but they'd given me money before and just couldn't anymore. We'd mortgaged our house as much as we could, and we were already behind two payments. I couldn't stop it; they canceled the insurance." Loretta took her hand away to cover her face. After a moment, she continued. "The hospital said they'd continue the treatments for awhile, just out of kindness. But my husband said that was charity. He turned them down. He was always so proud of being independent. Then he died. He'd been my whole life." She paused again and smiled sadly. "I guess I just went crazy. Somehow it all became T.D.'s fault. All his conniving and womanizing—it was just too much. We had a little pistol. I took it over to T.D.'s and shot him. I didn't say anything—just shot him. He was standing there in his back yard. It was like a dream. I left, went home and went to bed, must have slept for twelve hours. When I woke, it was almost like it hadn't happened." She straightened up in her chair, a proud woman. "I'm sorry I did it. I'm sorry for everything." She began to sob uncontrollably.

Ray got up to hold her, saying illogically, "Everything will be okay." Of course, it was not going to be okay. It was going to get worse. Much worse.

OK Journal

My View—Tommy Jacks

The first thing you learn about hornet's nests is to leave them to professionals. We amateurs should not—repeat, *not*—poke, prod or perturb them. Either you accept those cautions or you learn from the consequences, provided you survive.

Most accept such wisdom on looks alone, but there's always someone who doesn't get the point. Next thing you know, it's all ungovernable madness and wild pain. What's worse is if that someone is old enough to know better.

Republican U.S. Senate candidate Henry Blackman is half past old enough. But there he was, whacking like mad at one of the biggest nests there is, snickering all the way up until the first squadron of really big ones buzzed out to exact terrible vengeance.

For his part, the Rev. Robert S. Olsen only sounded disappointed to learn someone would do anything so ill considered. As for the rest of the state of Oklahoma, the stingers were out and busy.

So, maybe it's time to go over some fundamental rules with Henry, whose lumps still throb with a pain that may not go away in time for Election Day.

Never, but never, attack someone not only on, but anywhere near, the basis of their religion. Yes, in philosophical terms, religion and faith can be considered as distinct matters. But the distance between them is quite short—just a half sidestep, for some—because each has so much to do with the other. You presumed on that distance, and therein hangs the hornet's nest. You picked up a cheap broomstick and took a swing at it, in a way you'd never stand for if it was done to you.

And don't pull out that limp alibi about the advertising agency putting the commercial on the air without your OK. No one buys it, least of all the agency of Fuller and Bumgardner, which as we speak is mixing salt and kerosene to slather over your bumps in open court. You think it hurts now, just wait. They'll hear you howling all the way to Tulsa.

But, what's the use? We are all too familiar with Blackman and how he handles the merest whiff of criticism. Spewing appalling profanities on live television, for no provocation greater than being asked a couple of honest questions. Blaming unnatural catastrophes like the torching of an oil tank farm belonging to the company he once owned on some group that exists only on certain pieces of paper that came only from himself.

November is only about two and a half months away. Somebody needs to take Blackman's broomstick away, preferably for good. &

21
NEWS GATHERING

Tommy parked his pathetic Ford Fairlane at the curb in front of the imposing building that housed Joe Louongo's law office. It occurred to him that he should really look into how much money he made. Maybe he could afford a better car. Immediately he felt bad about thinking that. After an inner chuckle, he headed inside.

"Hello. Anyone home?" This happened before. He called out again; no answer. He saw no one, so he decided to wait. The full-size sofa appeared to be the best option for Tommy to sit while he waited. Before long, he was stretched out and snoozing.

"Who the hell are you? What the fuck are you doing sleeping in here?" The man asking those questions behind glaring eyes was huge—maybe three hundred pounds, most of it muscles. He wasn't someone you want to annoy.

"Sorry. Guess I fell asleep. I'm here to see Joe Louongo. You know where he is?"

"How the hell would I know where he is? How'd you get in here?"

Tommy squinted at him. "The door was unlocked."

"The hell it was. I locked it myself. Did you break in?"

Tommy sensed the guy might be so stupid he couldn't be

talked to. "Now, why would I break in just to take a nap and wait?"

That did seem to throw him off, although not much. "How the hell do I know?"

"Benny, it's okay. I know this guy." Louongo breezed past, patting Benny on his massive back. "He's a friend of mine. Tommy, come into my office."

Benny still looked confused.

"New bodyguard?"

"No. My idiot second cousin from Jersey. Got into some trouble, and my mother talked me into letting him come out here. It's been a nightmare. I'm gonna send him back; driving me nuts. Just dumb as a post. I dunno, maybe he was brain damaged as a kid or somethin'. Or all that weightlifting shit fucked up his brain. Anyway—was I expecting you?"

"No." Tommy was adjusting to Louongo having relatives and a mother. "Been trying to get hold of Tomas. I guess he's disappeared again. Wondered if you knew anything about it."

"Well yeah, probably. But you know he's my client, so I can't really tell you anything. But he's okay. At least I think he is." Louongo kind of shrugged.

"Is he cooperating with the FBI regarding Chuck Branson?"

"Ask all you want; I can't tell you. I *can* say he's no longer in legal jeopardy."

"Okay, so he's cooperating."

Louongo just looked at Tommy like they spoke different languages. Maybe this conversation needed to be over.

Tommy headed to the *Oklahoma Sun*. If Louongo wouldn't talk, maybe his dad would.

"You do know we work for competing papers, right?" Ray

grinned at giving his son a hard time.

"Look, I'm not asking for secrets. I just wondered if you knew what was happening with T.D. McFadden's murder. I heard they arrested his office manager. Didn't she use to work for you?"

"You should ask her attorney."

"Who's that?"

"Joe Louongo."

"You've got to be kidding. I was just in his office and he didn't mention it. He wouldn't tell me anything about anything. Why would a normal person hire Louongo?"

"Because she's charged with the very not-normal crime of murder. Who better?"

"Yeah, maybe so." Tommy admitted glumly. "Is the *Sun* still not going to endorse anyone for Senate?"

"You're not looking for filler for your columns, are you?"

He slumped. "No dad, just conversation—my god."

Ray smiled. "As far as I know, no. Blackman's probably starting to look better especially since I'm sure Robbie's not in favor of the preacher. At least Blackman's more or less a normal politician—corrupt, greedy, and pompous. Not sure about Olsen. What do you think?"

Tommy shook his head. "Too close to call, at least for now. My hunch is it gets decided after something happens between now and election day—revelation, scandal, whatever. It's all too mixed up." Tommy was still a little surprised to have a grown-up conversation about politics with his dad. "Think they'll have debates?"

"We're hearing two camps want a debate and one doesn't. But we don't know who that one is. And we hear they don't want it televised. I think since the Nixon-Kennedy debate, all the candidates are nervous about live TV."

Tommy gave that some thought. "I bet the one against is Fillmore. I don't think Albright likes the idea of his intellectual candidate on the same stage with two showmen."

"You could be right. Might not be very informative, but it sure as hell should be entertaining." Ray's silly grin reminded Tommy of his dad's drinking days.

"See you tonight. We're bringing hamburgers." Tommy headed out.

Next stop, the Lawrence Alexander Law Offices where Patsy worked for her uncle.

"Well, well. Are you being more attentive or just spying on me?" Patsy looked absolutely beautiful.

And Tommy was deeply in love. "I could say I was just in the neighborhood and needed to borrow a dollar. But maybe it would be best if I said I couldn't stay away another minute." Tommy gave her a quick kiss, making sure no one was around to see.

"You can have your dollar if I can get another kiss." Invitation accepted. "Okay, now tell me why you came here."

"Out on my rounds, seeing Dad and Louongo. So, seemed like a good opportunity to stop by and gawk at you."

Patsy blushed. "Whatever happened to the shy Tommy?"

"He fell in love." Tommy grinned his dad's silly grin. "Guess I'll head back to the capitol. Remember, tonight we're going to Tracy's and dad's with burgers."

"Sure." Patsy was smiling, everything seemed good. "I know I shouldn't tell you this, but your buddy Louongo called Uncle Larry this morning. Don't know what about."

"Wow. Can't imagine them having any connections at all." Tommy said goodbye with another quick kiss and headed out, thinking about two lawyers from the opposite ends of the universe and what they could be talking about. Out of habit he took Classen even though Broadway would have been quicker. Realizing that, he pulled in at Denny's just in case.

"Looky here. It's the roving boy reporter, Tommy Jacks," Albright announced from the booth shared with the always fashionable Max and Nathan.

Tommy was sure Albright had few friends because he was so annoying. Of course, he was sitting with his two New York pals, so maybe some people found him charming or something. "Good to see you, too, Taylor." Tommy nodded to Max and Nathan.

"What brings you to the lovely confines of Denny's?"

Tommy answered with a question, "Is Fillmore going to join the Senate debate or opt out?"

"A direct question deserves a direct answer: how the hell would I know?" Albright and his pals grinned.

"So, you're sticking with the story that you aren't running Fillmore's campaign?"

"It's not a story, it's the truth. And I always stick with the truth."

"Okay, you win that round. But just as a politically astute observer, do you think the three candidates should have a debate?" Maybe he could get something.

"Of course. The voters always have a right to hear what these people think and what they might do. Especially in this case, it's extremely important. None of the three have held office before. The debate may be the only opportunity to actually get a sense of who each candidate is and what he might do if he wins."

A quote from Albright wouldn't have much meaning for his readers since he had no official capacity with the campaign. But he had a point. Choosing between Blackman, Olsen, and Fillmore was a big gamble for the voter. The more information, the better.

"I agree. So, I think the debate will happen. And I think Fillmore's probably running third and stands to lose the most if he chooses not to debate."

"I don't disagree. That preacher has really thrown a monkey wrench into the whole thing." Albright didn't look happy. That said a lot about Fillmore's chances.

Tommy's next stop was the capitol press room, his sanctuary almost from his first day with the *Journal*. He wasn't sure he would have survived those first months if he hadn't had a place to hide from his "sort-of" bosses then, while he was a stringer. He was so new, and so scared and unsure of himself, he'd have panicked and left if he'd been in the newsroom. The press room was seldom used when the Legislature wasn't in session. He took comfort in its familiar surroundings. He was concentrating on writing when the phone rang.

"Press room. Jacks."

"Tommy? Vince. Fitzgerald just called and said he got some background scuttlebutt from one of his police contacts. He said they have evidence pointing to Ed Black in the murder of Buck Howard, and they have a warrant for him. But he's disappeared. He hasn't been seen since he left a Bixby hospital after he got beat up in some dive."

"That isn't a complete surprise. Any mention of Blackman?"

"Nope. Fitzgerald said they can't connect Blackman to Black, so it's just him they're looking for."

Tommy thought how interesting an interview with Mister Black could be. "Hasn't he been Blackman's sidekick for years?"

"Yeah, they go way back. I've heard from others, like Dick, that most people at Connex thought he was capable of every terrible thing you could think of. Why Blackman kept him around was a mystery."

"Maybe he knew too much." Tommy thought that made a lot of sense.

22
SATURDAY AGENDA

Tommy woke to the phone ringing. Patsy had spent the night, so he quickly answered—of course, too late. She squinted at him.

"Hello."

"Tommy. Sorry to wake you. We had a great night last night. Be sure and tell Patsy how much we love her."

"Tracy. You called at five o'clock in the morning to tell me you had a great night?"

"Of course not. The producer just found out the Reverend Olsen would like to appear on our show for an interview and wants to do it in two hours. Can you be here?"

Tommy had become more comfortable with the live interviews but having no time to prepare didn't feel right. "What's the rush?"

"Don't know. The producer just got the call, and he asked me to call you. Normally I don't even do the Saturday show, but the weekend host woke up this morning sick as a dog, so here I am. If you're not ready, or not comfortable, just say no. They'll just reschedule. It's not you causing the problem. It's the Olsen guy having his people call in the morning and wanting to be on TV right now. I'll just tell them you can't do it."

"What if they ask you to interview him?"

"Guess they could. I could just ask him simple questions

and let him talk."

Tommy wanted to interview Olsen, but not on such short notice. He thought a minute. "I'll do it. It'll take me about an hour to get dressed and get there. But I'll be there."

Tommy gave Patsy a kiss on the forehead. "Tracy says she loves you, and so do I." He smiled. She smiled. "Hi ho, hi ho, it's off to work I go."

The annoying weekday producer also was the annoying weekend producer. "The reverend just called. They're about fifteen minutes away. You ready?"

"As ready as I'll ever be."

Reverend Olsen and his entourage arrived, cramming fifteen more people into the crowded studio. Tommy took his spot in front of the camera while the reverend was powdered and brought up.

"We'll do two segments, both lasting right at six minutes. I'll ask you a few questions and you can take what time you need to answer. Of course, the longer your answer on one question, the less time we have for other questions."

"I understand, son." Olsen's tone was fatherly—maybe biblical.

"We're very pleased to have as our special guest this morning the Reverend Robert Olsen, who besides being a well-known minister and televangelist, is running for the U.S. Senate as an independent candidate. Welcome, Reverend Olsen."

"Thank you, Tommy. I want to thank KVY for accommodating me this morning and allowing me to appear with you to discuss the senate race and its importance to all of Oklahoma."

His voice had magically gone up a notch in volume and an octave lower. Tommy was impressed and opened his questions in his usual squeaky voice. "As a minister running for public office, one of the issues that's been raised by some, including your opponents, concerns your commitment to your religion and whether that's a conflict with your representation of all people's interests in Congress. Do you believe you can represent all people, even ones who don't have the same religious beliefs that you do?"

"This is a religious country," Olsen replied evenly. "The founders were religious people who respected all types of religion. I can and I will represent all people, whether they're Baptist, Catholic, or Pentecostal. I'll respect those differences while achieving accomplishments to make the lives of all Oklahomans better."

"What about people who aren't religious?"

"Well, son, 'bout all I can do for those people is pray. No sense in me saying I'll respect their views, because I won't. A lack of belief in God is no belief at all and the work of the devil. My work in Congress will be for the good, God-fearing people of Oklahoma, no matter their religion."

"Let me be sure I understand. You're saying you won't represent people who are atheists?"

"That's correct. I'm a man of God, and being a senator won't change that. As I said, I'll pray for those people and hope they can see the truth and become one with our Lord."

"Do you believe the United States was founded on the principles of being a secular society?"

Olsen frowned. "Of course not. What rubbish. What kind of question is that, anyway? Everyone knows this nation was established as a religious country with belief in one God. The founders made it clear this country was based on a Christian belief, and that hasn't changed. What has changed is that a lot of liberal-thinking people have lost their way and believe that man can just do as he wishes without consequences. But that's not true. God's watching, and it's time we get back to the right way of living."

"There is no mention of God in our Constitution. As a matter of fact, the only mention of religion was that 'no religious test shall ever be required as a qualification to any office.' How would you interpret that part of the Constitution?"

"I interpret it just like everybody else. It doesn't matter what religion you are; you can hold public office. I sure don't interpret it as meaning an atheist can hold office. That just isn't true."

Tommy looked to the camera, prompted by the producer. "We'll take a short break and be right back."

As soon as they were clear, Olsen blustered at him. "What kind of silly-ass questions are you asking? I came here to talk issues related to the senate race, not discuss how to interpret the Constitution. What are you, some kind of atheist?"

"I thought they were issues pertinent to your campaign, and you'd want to talk about them. I'm not trying to make you angry."

"Well, you better get on to something that matters, or you'll be sitting here alone."

Tommy wasn't sure he could ask this guy a question that was not loaded with some religious issue. It was all that was coming to him. On the other hand, he didn't want to run off another senate candidate. He was given the signal that they were coming back from commercial.

"Welcome back. Our guest today is Reverend Robert S. Olsen, who's running for the U.S. Senate. Reverend, have you agreed to debate your opponents?"

"Yes, we've reached an agreement—actually only yester-day—to have a debate. It'll be in two weeks, in the media center on the campus of Oklahoma State University in Stillwater. It won't be televised due to the objections of one of the candidates—not me, I should add. I expect it'll be a lively debate and will give all voters a chance to hear directly from the candidates as opposed to some newsperson's slanted opinion."

Tommy cleared his throat at that, but asked, "One of the big issues in Oklahoma is farm policies and the support provided by the federal government to farmers throughout the state. What are your positions on those issues?" He just handed Olsen that one. No doubt whatever he was saying was well scripted and of zero substance. He was happy to let the reverend drone on while he decided how to wrap it up.

"Thank you, Reverend, that was very helpful. My last question goes back to our earlier discussion of religion. The first amendment to the Bill of Rights states, 'Congress shall make no law respecting an establishment of religion, or prohibiting free exercise thereof,' which was later paraphrased by Thomas Jefferson as a 'separation of church and state.' Is your candidacy in any way a violation of that basic aspect of our constitution?"

The reverend glowered, perhaps trying to make up his mind if he would answer or leave. "The question is a legitimate one. I'm a religious man. I'm a minister. I'm a man of God. While it may give pause to some, I don't believe there's anything in our founding documents that prohibits a man, such as myself, who is religious and believes completely in God, from serving in public office. I'll try my best to represent all people and work to make their lives better. That's all I can do."

"Thank you, Reverend Olsen, for being with us today. Back to you, Tracy."

The reverend still looked bothered, but his face softened. "I don't know if you were trying to trap me or not. But maybe that was a good interview. I know those issues about my religious beliefs are out there, and I have to deal with them." He stood with Tommy and shook his hand, holding it for a little too long. And then he and his many followers left. Everyone in the studio let their breaths out.

"Best fucking interview we've ever had. How do you do this shit? It's just great." The producer seemed happy.

Tracy came over and gave Tommy a hug. "That was good, especially on such short notice. You know, I'm starting to think the Reverend may have a chance. What about you?"

He nodded. "You can tell he's smart. And he's learning."

In a surprise move, because it was yet early in the campaign, the *OK Journal* was about to publish its endorsement of Howard Fillmore.

The editorial read,

> *"Today we proudly endorse the best candidate to represent our diverse state in the U.S. Senate: Howard Fillmore. His years as an educator and president of one of the most prestigious private schools in the state provide him with a level of intellect and understanding that will position this great state to reach new and bigger accomplishments. There is no one of greater character and ethical beliefs running for this position of high trust than Mister Fillmore. He will work tirelessly for all Oklahomans,*

not only the few that meet his standards. Oklahoma needs a leader in our nation's chambers who can express with a clear vision what is important to our continued success and prosperity. We urge you to cast your vote for the best man in the race: Howard Fillmore."

"What did you think of that?" Vince had brought a copy to Risso's for Tommy to read over an afternoon beer. It would appear in the next day's paper.

"Well, you can sure see the shots at Olsen and Blackman. He has my vote, but I don't know if he's exciting anyone else. All I hear about is Olsen and Blackman. It's like Fillmore's an also-ran."

"Yeah. My father-in-law, no political genius, says he expects Olsen to win because of all of the religious people in the state." Vince sipped his beer and tried to relax. The *Journal* had been reducing staff, and to make things worse, people were quitting over the pressure of extra work like Vince carried. He looked tired.

"I know. I hear the same. But a lot of those religious people don't necessarily want their minister to run the country. They want someone who can get things done—pass laws, work with other legislators. Olsen definitely would be a great speaker, but does he know how to compromise, craft legislation, and run a functioning office? I don't know. People want senators who get things done. They want a preacher to preach."

23
LIFE AND DEATH

Life in the shadows was natural for Chuck Branson. He found a desperate grace among the so-called "lowlife" street people but never with average, upstanding citizens. His mother always told him, "You'll never amount to anything." Of course, she'd never amounted to anything, so maybe she knew. He joined the Air Force right after graduating from high school, and she died a few years later from chain-smoking and drinking. He didn't go to her funeral.

He'd had a good run of being more than she expected in the Air Force and almost normal working on the base newspaper. The biggest surprise was getting on at the *OK Journal.* He applied for the police beat job on kind of a lark. He lied on his application and expected to be turned down, but those schmucks were so confused getting started and checked out little to nothing. He was good at the job. He wasn't much of a writer, but the stories were all short, usually just lists of facts. If a story needed to sound better, the editor would rewrite it and never say a thing to him. He mingled in the world he knew, and it was where he was most comfortable. He was treated like one of them. He didn't mind.

Reno Avenue in downtown Oklahoma City had cheap hotels that suited him fine. It was a good place to be while he worked on a plan. It was likely that Matt already talked to the feds or the cops and the package and the money were gone. But he had to know. It was too important to his escape plan to forget about it. He'd thought about it during the torturous bus ride through the whole damned state of Texas. He decided the one person who might know about his cousin and the money might be someone he could find—Tommy Jacks.

He knew Tommy mostly hung out at the press room in the capitol, but he didn't know what to do once he found him. If things went wrong, he couldn't escape by taking a city bus that stopped at almost every corner. Would he have to use his gun to keep him in check? If so, could they just walk out? What made sense was to get Jacks down to his world; meet him somewhere in lowlife land. Of course, he might just call the cops instead. But he knew if Jacks thought there was a story, he'd come. He was a good reporter, just not very bright.

"Press room. Jacks."

"Hey, Tommy. It's your old pal, Chuck."

Tommy turned pale. He slowly sat down. "Chuck. I'm—I'm pretty sure you should call the police and turn yourself in." He fought the impulse to hang up.

"It's all bullshit," Chuck replied, doing his best to make everything sound minor. "I didn't do anything. They just gotta find someone to blame for this shit. I don't even know what they're sayin', but I'm sure it's a bunch of lies. Sure, I was involved for a while with those drugs out of South America. But that was small-time, and my so-called partner split and took all that as his own ages ago. I'm not even sure I did anything wrong except maybe somethin' to do with the Air Force. But listen—I know lots of stuff. Things about Big Frank Martin, things about that crooked police chief Underwood. I need some help, Tommy, and I can sure give you one hell of a story. I just need you to loan me a hundred bucks. That's all. Once I tell you all I know, I'm gettin' on a bus to Mexico. I'm tellin' you, I didn't do anything wrong, and I sure as hell didn't hurt anyone."

Tommy only wanted him to go away. "You're in trouble, Chuck. You should just turn yourself in. I can't do anything."

"Well, thanks a lot, asshole. I'm offering you a good story, and for a lousy hundred bucks you're just gonna throw me to the wolves." There was a long minute of silence. "How's my cousin Matt Tomas doin'?"

"He told me you were his cousin, but he's disappeared. Did you have anything to do with that?" Tommy thought about hanging up and calling the FBI. But what would he tell them? That he talked to Branson but he doesn't know where he was or where he was going and he wanted a hundred bucks? Great information.

"Hotshot reporters *do* stick together. No, I had nothing to do with that. I was helping him with money—and, yeah, that's really bad of me, helping my cousin. Just get me some money, and I'll be gone. Come on, I need some help."

Tommy hung up, and right away everything felt wrong. He should have given him the money or set him up some way for the cops. He sat waiting for the phone to ring. But would he answer it? He felt meek, helpless, and lousy. He stayed put. The phone didn't ring. He realized Chuck knew where he was. He had to leave.

It was one of those very late summer days with only a touch of fall in the air, normally a favorite time of year, but he was thinking too hard and fast even to notice on the way to his car.

"Don't do anything stupid, and I won't shoot you."

Tommy knew the voice. He turned slowly to see Chuck pointing a silvery pistol at him. "I don't have any money."

"Get in." Chuck whipped around to the passenger seat. "Drive."

Tommy headed down 23rd. He'd never felt so scared. "What are you going to do?"

"First, we're going to get all the money you have in your bank account. If you don't, I'll shoot you. If you make any kind of scene in the bank, I'll shoot you and whoever's in the bank. Just do what I tell you, and maybe you'll live." Chuck spoke slowly, glaring at him.

"Okay." He drove to his bank on Penn off 23rd. To keep calm, he started figuring out how much he had in his account—maybe about seven hundred. He was glad to give it to Chuck if he'd just go away.

Inside the bank, Chuck whispered to leave a little in the account so the teller wouldn't get suspicious. Tommy asked the teller for his balance: seven hundred and eighty-three dollars. He requested seven hundred and fifty in cash. She gave him an annoyed look, which he hoped meant she suspected something; but it was only because he hadn't filled out the proper form, which she gave him to sign. She counted out the money and put it into a bank envelope. Transaction done. No alarm. No nothing. Business as usual.

Back in the car, Tommy's worry level hit a peak. What now?

"Get back on 23rd and head west. Once you get to Portland, get on Route 66 and keep going west." Chuck stuffed the cash into his jeans.

"What's going to happen?"

"Just drive and shut up."

Tommy had just filled up with gas, so even stopping for that wasn't an excuse. Plus, his car had a huge tank and got strangely good mileage—they could ride for hours. They passed Yukon on the way to El Reno.

"When you get to El Reno, get on the interstate."

Minutes turned into hours.

Finally, Chuck relaxed a bit. "You might as well tell me what happened with Matt. It won't make any difference in what happens to you, and I'm not coming back. So, the little creep's safe. What'd he do?"

That didn't make Tommy feel like telling him much. "He was supposed to have some dirt on Blackman to tell me about. But he disappeared."

"Was that at the convention at the Skirvin?"

"Yeah. Thought I saw you there. Were you?"

"I'll ask the questions. When did you see him again?"

"A couple of weeks later. He called to say he needed help. Mentioned you and a package."

"So, where's the package?"

"He gave it to the FBI, I think."

"Fuck." Chuck fell silent.

They crossed the border into Texas without any further conversation. Chuck seemed lost in his thoughts. A road sign said the next exit was McLean. He looked up. "Pull off here. I gotta piss. We should get gas."

At the pump, Chuck grabbed Tommy's arm. "You can cause trouble here and you'll be the first person shot. Take care of your business, no mistakes, and we're back in the car and nobody's hurt. Got it?"

An hour later the road signs indicated they were getting close to Amarillo. An airport lay to the north. Chuck gestured to take the exit onto a two-lane road with no traffic, then a dirt road that seemed to go nowhere. Tommy's anxiety climbed.

"Stop."

He was going to kill him. There was no rush of thoughts. Just fear. And sweat.

Chuck must have noticed. "Relax. I'm not going to kill you," he said evenly. "Believe it or not, I'm not a killer. Yeah, I might've killed Matt, but he's family. He shouldn't have screwed me out of my money. It was all I wanted. I knew there was a lot of other stuff in the package. But how the hell was I supposed to get to the Cayman Islands and walk into some high-class, rich-guy bank and cash out without every cop in the world waitin' for me? All I wanted was the cash to get away. I was never a big part of that mess in Oklahoma City. That was Martin and Jenkins and that crazy police chief. I was just on the edges, tryin' to make a little." He sighed. "Anyway, thanks for the money—and unfortunately, the car. You're a success; you'll just get another. Me, I've got no choice. I always liked you, Tommy, so—sorry."

Chuck kept the gun pointed at Tommy while he got out and walked to the driver's side. They looked at each other for a few seconds. Tommy slowly moved out of the car and allowed Chuck to get in. With no further comment Chuck sped down the dirt road toward the highway.

The immediate release of tension was overwhelming. His knees buckled as he kneeled on the dirt road. All he could do was laugh—out loud and with complete joy. He'd never felt more alive. The air, the sky—it was all so beautiful. Life was wonderful.

Walking to the highway he couldn't stop smiling. Soon an old man in a pickup came by and offered him a lift. It was a short ride to the nearest truck stop. Tommy called the police. The cops showed up quickly. They got basic information from him and called it in. After that they seemed to be waiting on something. In a short amount of time two plain black Ford sedans pulled up with two FBI agents inside each. Tommy told them his story from an air-conditioned back seat, and once they heard Agent Swartz from Washington was in charge of matters connected to Branson, they became much more official. They drove him to downtown Amarillo.

They put him in a room with a phone and instructions to call and let people know he was okay. Tommy called his dad. Ray pitched a fit and wanted to come and pick him up. Tommy said no. He asked Tommy if he thought he needed an attorney. No, he didn't. He told his dad he would call the paper, and once he knew exactly what was going to happen, he'd call him back. The next call was to Patsy, but she wasn't in the office and didn't answer her home phone. He called the *Journal.*

"Kidnapped? My God, Tommy. Are you all right? Where are you? How can we help?"

Tommy gave June the short version and said that as soon as he could he'd write a column.

The agent returned. "Agent Swartz wants to meet with you tomorrow in Oklahoma City to discuss what happened. We'll take you there. But I'm sure you need a few things prior to that."

The FBI agents treated him like a celebrity, which he liked.

They bought him a pair of jeans, a shirt, and some underwear at one of Amarillo's collection of western wear stores. Tommy was in the mood to shop for more, but it seemed inappropriate under the circumstances.

The local agents were very polite and concerned about his comfort. One asked, "I'm sure you're tired, but is there anything else we can do for you now?"

Tired wasn't the word, it was more like exhausted. Still, before the agents left he asked for a pen and paper. His need to keep notes was a habit hard to break.

Once the agents left, Tommy called his dad again and gave him an update. Then he asked if Tracy could call Patsy and let her know what was going on because he hadn't been able to reach her. His dad said that of course she would and told Tommy he loved him. That embarrassed Tommy a little, but made him smile.

Room service hamburgers are the best. He ordered one and settled in to write his column. One hell of a day.

OK Journal

My View—Tommy Jacks

In newspapers these days, you hear a lot about the trend toward specialization. One writer only does theater reviews. Another only writes sports. And another just covers politics.

We buck the trend at the *Journal.* If you work for us, come ready to write about whatever happens.

That means just because I mostly write about politics, even if that careens sometimes over into other topics like, say, murder, I can certainly strut my travelogue stuff, too.

From Oklahoma City to the outlying eastern suburbs and industrial parks of Amarillo, Interstate 40 slithers for close to 250 miles.

As for scenery, let's just say that past a certain point—and it's hard to say exactly where that is—everything looks like what you just drove past. That goes on for several miles after you cross the border into the Texas stovepipe where each mile is long because they don't do anything small there, even if it might save time and road fatigue. And forget about radio reception. KOMA breaks up and mutters out somewhere between Sayre and Erick, and from there on it's all nasal twang and pedal steel guitars.

A trip like that comes of unexpected and unbidden detours, and the facts will come out someday, provided I live longer than some people want me to. Let's just say I have official assurance that I will be returned to the humid bosom of Oklahoma City in just as many pieces as when I left. Wouldn't mind taking to this road again, but next time I won't be in such a hurry.

I mean I've just got to stop off at the Cherokee Trading Post out by Clinton. I lost count of how many bargains I missed, according to the billboards set every one-eighth mile up to and far past it. I've been daydreaming about how good a pair of authentic Indian moccasins would feel on my aching feet. &

24
DEBATE THE DEBATE

Tommy continued to cover the campaign, but he didn't push as hard as before. Surveys showed lead changes depending on factors that were never clear, maybe because of polling techniques. A few said the race was a three-way tie. Most said Olsen was the leader. Differences fell well within the margins of error.

Fillmore's campaign had the most trouble raising money. The usual Democratic contributors sensed a loss and didn't kick in as much. The Republicans' most loyal contributors also hesitated to bet on Blackman, but oil industry tycoons had plenty of money, and so did he. Raising money was second nature for Olsen, and his campaign seemed to have enough to do whatever it liked.

The loss of Tommy's beloved ugly wreck of a car was an emotional sore spot. It was found abandoned at the bottom of a ravine in New Mexico, a total wreck, and no sign of Chuck. With Ray's help he got a deal on a 1960 Chevy Impala, black with red interior. He liked it, even if the fins were a little much. Patsy thought it was "fab." Rather than look dumb, he didn't ask if that was good or bad.

They took a couple of day trips to state parks and other tourist spots for more one-on-one time to learn about each other. It became clear that most of what he talked about was politics or newspapers while Patsy seemed interested in every-thing. He enjoyed listening to her voice. Her one-sided con-versations were fine with him.

"I guess you'll be going to the debate in a few days." Patsy bringing up politics indicated she was trying to get him to talk.

"Yeah. Could be entertaining. Want to come?"

"Sure. How do you think it will turn out?" She tried to seem interested in his political world.

"The strongest speaker is Olsen. He's a natural. You could say it's because he's a preacher, but he knows how to connect with people. He should have a good debate unless the ques-tions irritate him—and then he can get angry fast. But he's been practicing; he's more polished. If he'll stick to politics and stay away from preaching, he'll do all right." He shook his head. "But Blackman's a loose cannon. If he could just give a speech, he'd be fine. But the format has a moderator who asks questions. Blackman doesn't like that. He gets defensive. I once thought it was Fillmore who didn't want to debate, but now I think it was Blackman. If he loses his temper, he might say anything. Fillmore has the most to gain. Many people haven't heard him speak, and the format's perfect for him. He's thoughtful, doesn't attack people, and he's smart. That'll come across to people if they give him a chance."

"So you're predicting a toss-up?"

"I think Fillmore is the best man. He has no overriding ego and will work with anyone. But he's a liberal in a very conserva-tive state, which means he'll most likely come in third. Black-man's scary. I think most people can sense that and won't vote for him unless they're tied to the oil industry. So I think," he sighed, "the winner of the debate and the election will be Olsen."

"Even though he's said some pretty stupid things about non-religious people?"

"But most Oklahomans agree with him. He'll be a disaster as a senator. But I think he wins this time."

"Can't you help change that?"

He shook his head. "The impact of my opinion is zero. Electing lousy politicians is an American right—not spelled out in the Bill of Rights, but nonetheless, you just hope the bad ones don't outnumber the good ones."

Blackman sat at a conference table surrounded by attorneys, signing the final documents to sell Connex to Cook Oil. It was an amazing feat to avoid bankruptcy and humiliation. But he still felt like he was losing. Connex had been his creation. From nothing he'd built it into one of the major oil companies in the country. It gave him wealth, prestige, and power. He still had money, but all else was gone with the stroke of a pen. He signed the last document, then stood and shook Byron Cook's hand. "Thanks." He didn't mean it. The deal was the right thing, but it still felt like Cook somehow took advantage of his misfortune.

He'd cleared out his office at Connex and moved to his campaign headquarters a few blocks away. People there started bringing him things that needed his attention or approval. It was a struggle to stay focused on the race. And he'd never told anyone about his overriding sense of foreboding since Ed Black had disappeared. In some ways he wanted Ed out of his life, but in others he missed him. When he was told an arrest warrant was issued for Ed in the death of the state tank inspector, he felt a chill. He knew Ed killed the guy. He hadn't told him to do it, but there never had been any question, so much so he'd been shocked the cops were so dense they didn't figure that out right off. He figured the police followed an assumption that top-level executives of major oil companies didn't kill people. Now that Ed was gone and the law was after him, it posed a problem. He knew Ed wouldn't go quietly and he knew where the bodies were buried. Blackman didn't know what to do, but he knew something would happen soon.

"What needs to happen now to get our candidate to the senate?"

Mary Ann Peterson glowered at Albright like she was thinking of a nice way to tell him to go to hell. "You know there's no magic wand. You have to win the most votes. So I guess your question is, do I have a plan to win more votes than Olsen and Blackman? The answer is no." Mary Ann smiled at Taylor tightly. "Realistically, our only chance is the debate. Olsen and Blackman are outspending us almost two to one, so we won't win the advertising battle. Most one-on-one interviews are going to Olsen, with Blackman a close second. We're doing interviews with the editor of the *Enid Daily*. It isn't a pretty picture. Do *you* have an answer?"

Albright sighed. "You're right. But our only chance really is if it is televised live. Maybe Blackman knew that, but I really think he didn't want a TV debate because he thought it would help Olsen most. Either way, he may have sunk our campaign."

"Wow, did someone die?" Howard Fillmore walked into the gloom. "Oh, I get it—you're discussing my chances of winning." He laughed. "Listen, don't get down on yourselves.

That was never expected. I thought if, and that was a big 'if,' I could win the Democratic primary, I'd have a chance, with the *Journal's* endorsement. But I'd never figured on an independent candidate with statewide appeal and lots of money. If I'd known that, I could've told you there was no way I could win. So, cheer up. We're getting close to the end, and then we can all go back to what we were doing."

Albright did not give up that easily. "We were talking about the debate being the best hope. If you have a good showing, it could decide the race."

Howard sighed with a smile. "Taylor, you know that isn't true. Even if I had the best debate performance ever given by a candidate, the impact would not be enough to change things. Everything points to me coming in third with about twenty-five percent of the vote, and either of the other two winning by a few percentage points. What I really hate is that I don't think either one of them can be a good senator."

Albright sat up. "You've got to make that exact point in the debate. These guys are blowhards, but they have no substance." Albright looked happier for a minute, but it went away as quickly as it came. "I know. So what? That's what the voter wants: someone to wave their arms and shout. Who cares about the hard work of producing results?"

Howard nodded. "Mary Ann, I think we need to consider the debate our last hurrah. Let's spend whatever money we have on hand in the next few days. Run some of those new commercials you produced, and ads in both major markets as much as our cash will allow. We'll worry about what to do next later. What do you think, Taylor?"

"Well, I do like those new commercials. Good job, Mary

Ann." Albright smiled at her. She was almost too nice a person to be in politics. "Go all-out and see what happens." He thought, *what happens is, you lose. Another fine job done by the oh-for-two campaign guru from the famous city of New York. Maybe my book'll be a short story.*

OK Journal

My View—Tommy Jacks

I'm wearing those moccasins. You know, the ones I told you I had my eye on ever since I passed that billboard west of Clinton on Interstate 40, done up in bright, fresh mustard yellow with fire engine red letters tall as giraffes. "Authentic," they spelled out in an arch over a picture of them, size 1200, width E to the twentieth power.

"Indian made," the billboard assures us. It could have added, "Cheaper than the Genuine Bowie Knife on the next billboard," but that's poor marketing. Anyway, that's probably the main reason why I have them instead of the "Real" bone-handled Bowie knife, which I kind of wanted. Besides, the person who paid for my moccasins was afraid I'd cut my thumb off, or worse.

As for the moccasins, I like them fine. They do make me wish I'd paid more attention for that six minutes out of three years I spent in junior high while one of my teachers covered Native American culture and crafts. Maybe if I had, I could tell whether they're really "Authentic" and "Indian Made."

There's no sense in buyer's remorse or consumer suspicion. They're strongly advertised as comfortable, and the proof, as they say, is in the wearing. So, I tried them on before my Bowie knife-averse companion peeled the bills for them.

In kind of the same way, voters will get to try out the three candidates for U.S. Senate at next week's event at the media center at Oklahoma State University in Stillwater. Republican Henry Blackman, Democrat Howard Fillmore and the Rev. Robert S. Olsen, an independent, will answer questions posed by a moderator, although, so far, we don't know whether they'll do so on live television or radio.

If they don't debate live, the result will be kind of like having to decide whether to buy moccasins after hearing someone else describe trying them on. It might work, but only *might*.

I'm not about to say there shouldn't be a debate for that reason any more than I'd say you should drive out for a pair of these moccasins on my word alone.

I'm just putting in that whoever decided not to televise or broadcast it live isn't giving voters in this state nearly as much to go on as they deserve. ❦

25

TELEVISION DRAMA

Oklahoma City and Tulsa TV stations approached the campaigns to ask again to televise the Senate campaign debate live. In a surprise move, all three agreed. It was an end run because they went to each campaign, which meant bypassing the League of Women Voters, who organized the debate. It turned out to be a smart move. No one wanted to be the camp that objected. The anxiety and excitement turned up a notch.

"Who's the moderator?" Patsy asked Tommy on the way there.

"Television guy from Tulsa. Mack something-or-other. Probably softball questions with time to expand if the candidate wants. They'll make opening and closing statements. And they can't address each other directly."

"Sounds civil. And boring."

"Yeah. But you never know what might happen." Tommy suspected Blackman and Olsen thought rules were for other people.

The media center on the OSU campus was a new building, seated about three hundred, and was expected to be full. Prefect for live TV coverage. It put focus on the candidates.

Tracy was the first person they noticed inside the center. Patsy gushed about how nice Tracy looked.

Tracy thanked Patsy but seemed pre-occupied. "These unscripted things make me nervous. You never know what might happen."

"Do you have to do much?" Patsy asked.

"Not really. We have a thirty-second introduction, and then shift to the moderator. There'll be a break at the halfway point, I'll do a close, and then we send it back to the studio where they'll do the analysis. The hard part will be staying awake." Tracy gave one of her knockout smiles. They could tell she was on edge.

Patsy and Tommy found their seats near the front. "I think these were supposed to be Mister Anderson's," Tommy told her, "but he decided not to come. He endorsed Fillmore, so maybe he thought it wouldn't look good."

An official from the League of Women Voters came on stage to discuss decorum with a stern, teacher-like tone, instructing the audience that no applause or any other visible or audible indication of support or disapproval would be allowed aside from greeting the candidates at the beginning, and then only briefly.

Mack something-or-other introduced the candidates, and each gave a three-minute opening statement with no surprises. The first question went to Fillmore.

"Doctor Fillmore, you've been described as a liberal. How would you classify your political philosophy?"

"Might as well get this out of the way—I'm not a communist." Fillmore smiled to gentle, supportive laughter. "I've always believed in a small, efficient government, but also I do believe in a government that's involved with its citizens and helps—"

"Communist bastard! All you want is to take over this country and take away our freedoms—everything you say is a lie! If people knew what you wanted, no one would vote for you. You're a damn communist—"

Sheriff's deputies instantly surrounded a tall man who had risen to stand and shout in the middle of the audience. They all but carried him out of the auditorium. He kept shouting, but it was hard to tell what he said. The crowd sat, hushed and apprehensive.

Fillmore began again, "Sorry about that. Not one of my fans, apparently." The audience laughed a little louder, releasing the tension. "I know labels help us understand the world and how we fit into it, but ones like 'liberal' or 'conservative' are too glib for a complex idea. What I can say is that my only interest in being your senator is to be a benefit to the people of Oklahoma, and I'll work tirelessly to achieve that." There was a smattering of applause, even if not allowed. Fillmore took his seat.

The moderator asked Blackman about changes he would seek as a U.S. senator that would impact the oil industry. It seemed like a huge softball question, but it had meaning to a state so dependent on the industry. His answer was mostly taken from his stump speech about his background and how he was the only candidate who could fix the problems in Washington when it came to the punitive regulations forced on Oklahomans by anti-oil liberals. His remarks were clear and well-delivered.

The moderator turned to address Olsen. "Mister Olsen, I think most Oklahomans agree with you that it isn't wrong for a man of God to seek office. But can you tell us how your background will help you deal with the legislative process and get laws passed that'll benefit everyone in the state?"

With a booming voice that needed little amplification, Olsen was ready. "Thank you, Mack. Great to see you again. Well, as everyone knows I'm not a politician, which I think is a good thing." He paused with a preacher's smile. "But I know how to deal with people, so I believe I'll be able—"

A man ran down the aisle toward the stage. He held a large-caliber pistol. About midway down, he fired, the noise was deafening in the small auditorium. He fired again. Most in the crowd hit the floor, and many were screaming. Four deputies appeared behind the shooter, yelling and aiming their weapons at the man. He turned toward them, and they fired. He was hit by multiple bullets, and dead before he fell backward to the floor.

Tommy popped his head up to look at the stage. The target had been Howard. He sat in a folding chair, hit in his upper chest. He didn't move, and he was losing blood fast. Blackman had been grabbed by his people and whisked offstage. Olsen seemed in shock. He sat on the floor, stunned but unhurt.

Emergency crews, firemen, and paramedics burst in. Two men were already attending to Fillmore. Tommy figured they might be doctors; they gave directions. People tracked his blood across the stage.

Some came to help Olsen off the stage. He seemed almost catatonic.

Fillmore was lifted onto a gurney and carted to a waiting ambulance.

"Are you okay?" Tommy helped Patsy up. The aisle was blocked by sheriff's deputies around the body of the shooter.

"I can't stop shaking." She was on the verge of tears. Tommy held her. He could see, in the back, cameras pointed at each station's reporter, each giving an account of what happened. Tracy was on the air. He shuddered. At least his father knew she was safe.

Police and deputies began ushering people out.

"Just a minute," Tommy told Patsy, "I need to say something to Tracy. You go on out, and I'll be there in a minute."

"Bullshit, I'm staying with you." She clung to him.

Tommy waved down Tracy. "I can hardly breathe in here," she sobbed.

"Let's get outside. You'll feel better." He reached for Tracy's hand.

In the cool night air, their color started to return. "I just hope Howard doesn't die," Tracy almost whispered. Maybe she was afraid to say it too loudly, in case the worst had already happened.

Tommy tried to reassure Tracy. "He's lost a lot of blood, but they were very quick to respond and treat him." After a brief pause he stated. "The shooter was the same guy who yelled at the beginning. I think I know who he is."

"How?" Tracy sounded worried.

"Louongo told me about him. His name's Thorsten Daniels. He's head of the Freedom Branch Society in Oklahoma. He's a dentist from Sapulpa. I saw him at every rally for Blackman I went to."

"The anti-communist people, right?" Tracy had regained her reporter focus.

"Yeah. The founder is Byron Cook—the guy who just bought Connex from Henry Blackman."

"Jeez, you don't think they're connected with this, do you?"

"No. I think Daniels did this on his own. I don't believe

Blackman or Cook wanted it."

Tracy hugged them both quickly. "I need to get back in. Are you headed home?"

"Yeah. Do you need us to wait on you?"

"No, I rode up here with the camera crew, and my car's at the station. We'll leave in just a minute. I'll call you when I get home. Be careful."

"Sure. You, too. I love you." He felt reluctant to leave but knew that was silly.

The drive home was mostly silent. There just didn't seem to be much to say.

OK Journal

My View—Tommy Jacks

John F. Kennedy in Texas. Robert F. Kennedy in California. Martin Luther King in Tennessee.

And now, politics by gunfire comes to Oklahoma.

We're awaiting word as to whether Howard Fillmore's name will be added to that list of men involved in politics or civil discourse killed by others whose vision never penetrated their private, self-serving sicknesses. We're praying not.

Even at that, the damage might be done.

Thorsten Daniels, who shot Fillmore, didn't live as long as Lee Harvey Oswald. A fusillade from Payne County deputies killed him in the middle of Oklahoma State University's media center after his second assault on last night's debate.

As you should have read elsewhere in today's edition, he at first disrupted the opening moments of last night's debate. The deputies wrestled him out but didn't seem to consider him a threat. They also didn't search for any weapons on him and, according to the latest information, let him go after he apologized and promised to behave.

But as soon as he went back inside, he opened fire, striking Fillmore in the chest.

I was in a front row, and dove to the floor after hearing that odd, sadly familiar slapping noise bullets make while they fly past. I saw Fillmore, who'd just begun to rise out of a folding chair on the small stage, sink backward to sit again, ominously still, blood spreading across his shirt.

The Rev. Robert Olsen, the independent candidate who'd

just stood to answer a question from the moderator, wasn't hit, but withered downward, his eyes locked in a distant, uncomprehending gaze of shock and terror while heavy pops of pistol fire punched through the shouts and screams. Those bullets didn't make it to the stage. They stopped at Thorsten Daniels.

Daniels was a dentist, which means his business was, or should have been, caring about people. He lived in Sapulpa, and was a member of the Freedom Branch Society. The society is known for what many call an ultra-conservative perspective on American government and policy. I'll only say I'm not exactly sure what "ultra-conservative" means.

As beyond the pale as the society might seem, nothing in any known information about it, or in its unhinged and rather imaginative propaganda, seems to support what Daniels did.

And if we point out that the society was founded and is led by Byron Cook, owner of Cook Oil and Gas Co., which recently purchased Connex from Republican Senate candidate Henry Blackman, it is to warn anyone not to draw conclusions from that. The facts connect Cook to Blackman, but only that far.

Blackman, who was swept off the stage after the shooting started, seemed as surprised and frightened as one would expect in the line of gunfire.

The race now becomes completely different. You can't say there was only one casualty—not so far. The work of one man now dead and unable to explain his madness may not be done yet. ❦

26
NOW WHAT

Howard Fillmore lay in critical condition in the intensive care unit at Baptist Hospital in Oklahoma City. He'd been taken there by helicopter during the night from Stillwater General. A spokeswoman at the hospital gave a brief update to reporters.

"Doctor Fillmore has been in a coma since the shooting. This is primarily due to his loss of blood. The doctors were able to stabilized the patient in Stillwater before he was transported here, but that loss alone has him in critical condition. The doctors are also concerned about internal bleeding, and surgeons will operate as soon as his vital signs stabilize. If there are further developments, we will make another announcement later today."

Blackman's and Olsen's campaign offices issued statements condemning the violence. They indicated their campaigns would go on hiatus until further notice, and they prayed for Fillmore's speedy recovery.

Even so, TV ads continued to run. When asked about them, the campaigns said they'd been scheduled and couldn't be stopped. The TV stations countered that wasn't true.

The Payne County Sheriff's Department released a statement identifying the shooter as Thorsten Daniels, a fifty-four-year-old male involved in several political movements including the Freedom Branch Society. They talked to his wife, who confessed she had no idea why he'd done such a thing. She claimed he wasn't a violent man and didn't own a gun. The sheriff's department confirmed Daniels was the same man who'd interrupted the beginning of the debate and was ushered out by deputies. Daniels calmed down and apologized. They released him because they believed his act was more a stunt than anything else. The department said it would investigate the deputies' actions and details would come later.

The Freedom Branch Society released a statement expressing shock at Daniels's actions. The group insisted that it rejected violence in all forms and had never advocated it. Cook stated, "I knew Mister Daniels, and there was never any indication he might do something like this. Maybe something went wrong in his life, and he just snapped." At a public appearance in Washington, D.C., before a regulatory body regarding the recent purchase of Connex by Cook Oil, Byron Cook was booed by members of the audience, and the chairman of the committee had the public gallery cleared. Whatever he had to say in the so called public hearing was not disclosed.

Tommy hadn't slept well. When Patsy got up to get ready for work, he did, too. He made coffee and got the morning paper. Vince hadn't been in Stillwater for the debate because he decided, with Fred's approval, to watch on TV and file his report based on the same view as most voters had. His reporting, as usual, was factual and concise. The only thing new to Tommy was a quote from a member of the clean-up crew interviewed on TV. He said Olsen looked "in bad shape" while being taken to his car almost an hour after the incident.

"Good morning." Patsy took more time than Tommy

thought necessary to get herself ready. She was so beautiful, without all the effort. "Any news?"

"Not really. Comment in Vince's article says the reverend was still in shock almost an hour later. Strange that he stayed so long. Think I'll take a quick shower and head on out to the capitol."

"Sure. I'll see you tonight."

The capitol was almost empty. No one to gossip with. He was surprised to find Vince Young at a desk in the press room.

"Hey. You sleep here last night?"

Vince might have jumped three feet. "Jeez, don't sneak up on me like that." He took a deep breath. "No. But had trouble sleeping. Thought this'd be a good, quiet place to work a little. This isn't your usual time, is it?"

"Couldn't sleep, either."

"I know. I was so bummed about the whole thing—and I wasn't there like you. Just can't understand."

Tommy sighed. "Daniels probably genuinely feared communists, thought they were going to make everyone prisoners, something like that. Put that with a personal anger against the world, and I guess you have a killer. Who, I'm sure, will be described by his friends, patients, and employees as a nice man, and they can't believe he did this." He frowned. "The person who should be held responsible is Cook. Based on what I know, he started this hate group to stop regulation of the oil industry. I'd bet you a ten-dollar bill Cook thought most of his followers were nut-jobs, but he used them anyway. He stoked them so he could pollute—now, there's the real evil. *And, no, you cannot quote me.*"

"What's next?"

Tommy exhaled. "The show must go on. In a way. It's an election for a federal office, but the state runs it. The governor could postpone voting under certain circumstances, but I don't think Evans would want to. That would put him at the center of the issue. If Fillmore dies, or if he's unable to run and agrees to it, the Democratic Party can pick someone else. Not sure on the timing, though. I think there've been cases where someone died close to an election and still won. In that case, the governor would appoint someone to fill the position until a special election could be held."

"Who do you think wins now, assuming he recovers?"

"If the public gets the whole story about who the shooter was, that'll cause a lot of problems for Blackman. He can try to distance himself from Daniels, but I'd guess it gets hung around his neck. If that happens, it's a two-person contest. Olsen will keep his core, no matter what. The winner will be the one who benefits the most from the drop-off. I believe that'll be Fillmore."

"You're the same guy who said Olsen a few days ago."

"Yep. Things change. Somebody goes up, somebody goes down. That's politics." Tommy enjoyed talking about politics in the abstract. It seemed more like sports than life and death.

Joe Louongo had made a good living representing the underbelly of society, beating the system. Almost all his clients were guilty of something, if not of whatever they were charged with. Innocent people with good hearts didn't hire him. Until Loretta Lynch. He was as knowledgeable about criminal law as anyone in the state, but his manner, his approach to judges, his whole life, didn't fit well with her. He knew her plea deal had to be based on diminished capacity, with the threat of insanity defense dashed in. Every D.A. in the country would hate the case because there was no way to win. Put the grieving, poor widow in prison for killing the scum who caused her husband's painful death or let her go scot-free because you didn't mind murder if it was for a good cause. What the D.A. would want is a plea deal—admit the guilt with little or no punishment.

But Louongo was worried. He wasn't a favorite of the D.A. Okay, the D.A. hated him. That was fine with people he usually represented because the D.A. was always going after the maximum punishment. Plea deals with known criminals weren't good PR.

Loretta Lynch needed representation that could deal with the D.A. while not calling him a fucking idiot. Louongo knew Lawrence Alexander, even if they traveled in different circles. Years ago, however, Louongo helped Alexander in a case involving the son of one of his best corporate clients. The kid was pure evil, so much that Louongo suspected he scared Alexander. Louongo handled the matter in his normal way, first telling the kid to shut the fuck up or he'd have one of his companions in jail slit his throat. The kid shut up. He was able to get the charge reduced based on some errors by police and got only probation. The kid violated it within six months. But that wasn't Louongo's fault.

He called Alexander and explained his situation with Loretta. Alexander, always the professional, asked about payment. All lawyers had this one common bond. Louongo explained the connection with Ray Jacks and that he was doing the case *pro bono.* To his credit, Alexander agreed and said he'd visit with Loretta the next day.

Louongo didn't join them. But he could imagine her relief. She always did seem a little afraid of him.

The magic of Larry Alexander worked wonders. Using Louongo's game plan of pleading down to manslaughter with diminished capacity and insanity defense as a hole card worked perfectly. They agreed to time served and six months at the state mental hospital for evaluation. If she was declared not to be a risk to society, she'd be released.

The legal system actually seemed to work for Loretta Lynch, with the help of Larry Alexander and his connections. T.D. McFadden might have disagreed.

OK Journal

My View—Tommy Jacks

Here we are in the eye of the hurricane. We've survived so far, but there have been casualties. Howard Fillmore, the president of Oklahoma Corinthian College and Democratic candidate for U.S. Senate, lies in a coma.

The Rev. Robert S. Olsen, the independent candidate for the same seat, left the scene in Stillwater visibly shaken and hasn't been heard from aside from a stated agreement with Republican candidate Henry Blackman to suspend their schedules of campaign events until we find out more about Fillmore.

And of course, Thorsten Daniels, the late dentist from Sapulpa whose attempt to kill Fillmore caused all this, will undergo an autopsy and similar investigative intrusions, mostly to figure out what drove him to such madness. He was a member of the Freedom Branch Society, headed by Byron Cook, who by coincidence purchased Blackman's Connex oil and gas firm some weeks ago, and who has made clear to all that the society doesn't hold with shooting people.

As hard as it is to feel cold-blooded about all this, some objective matters have to be brought up. If Fillmore can't continue, what happens? If Blackman and/or Olsen protest they didn't plan on being in a shooting gallery and opt out, what's to do?

Everyone hopes for Fillmore to recover and for all candidates to hold their courses. The more time passes in the eye before the back end of the hurricane—that is, election day itself—hits, the more likely that seems. But if not, without going into more detail than we have room for, the whole thing will likely wind up with Gov. Bud Evans.

It's a cinch the eye of the storm doesn't feel like a moment of calm to him. In short, some circumstances may present the option of postponing the election and asking former Gov. Rick Butler to stay on another year or so. Or Evans might have to appoint someone else, bound to be a Republican and therefore bound to make every Democrat in the state howl like cornered coyotes.

And if you're a political vampire, like some around here, you've got to be intrigued by how the whole picture of the Senate race either has changed or might change.

Before the primary, Blackman seemed the frontrunner. After the primary and before Stillwater, Olsen seemed to take the lead. Now, after a brief, terrifying moment, nothing seems predictable.

And here comes the back of the hurricane. ❦

27

BEGINNINGS AND ENDINGS

Blackman really knew nothing about politicking. His campaign manager was an annoying little creep who he suspected he would've strangled under different circumstances. But, because he didn't want to change horses at this point, he started spending more time at his mansion in south Tulsa's Forest Meadows. His household staff stayed away as much as possible, for good reason. He'd rail at them over the most minor things.

But on this day he enjoyed a whisky and water and waited for his attorney. He'd lost the legal team at Connex and had to hire a new man he could totally intimidate. Still, the young lawyer didn't know shit. He'd been recommended by people Blackman didn't trust. They'd insisted he was the next great legal mind in the state. He heard the doorbell and sat waiting for whatever news would come, no doubt bad.

"Mister Blackman, thanks for seeing me. I know you must be busy with the campaign and everything. I sure don't mean to interrupt your day." The attorney was actually shaking, visibly.

The man was a weasel. Why did he hire this jerk? "Just tell me what sort of fucking nightmare has happened now." Blackman gave him the evil eye.

"Yes. Yes, of course. I was notified by the U.S. Attorney this morning they've filed charges against you for tax fraud and stock fraud. He said that in deference to your position in the community they'll give you until tomorrow morning to turn yourself in to U.S. marshals at their downtown office. If you don't, they'll issue a warrant for your arrest."

Blackman just stared. "Is this serious or some kind of political bullshit?"

The lawyer cleared his throat nervously. "I don't have all the details yet. The tax fraud is based on your tax returns, personal and corporate. The stock fraud's about the offering you pulled. It says you lied about the assets when you filed. And the U.S. Attorney said they were attaching conspiracy charges to each count. That means they think they can prove you committed cover-ups in conspiracy with others. You could face twenty-five years in prison and your assets will be put at risk. I wouldn't be surprised if your bank accounts are frozen." The attorney seemed on the verge of fainting. His primary specialty was real estate law—not massive financial crime.

"You're obviously an idiot—get the fuck out of here. In case that isn't clear, *you're fired.*" Blackman stood up, fists clenched. The attorney stumbled out.

Sonofabitch, what a fuckin' mess. He had cash hidden all over the world, but he'd grown old and slow. Could he get out? How could this happen so fast and he wasn't aware? It suddenly dawned on him: Ed Black. That bastard had to be spilling his guts. He slammed his fist on his desk, then gulped down his whisky. "Sonofabitch! Ed, you fucking bastard, you're dead!"

You had to be pretty dedicated to get hold of Louongo on the phone. He answered when he wanted, which wasn't usually. It seemed an odd practice for someone who asked people to call him for emergencies. But he had a system. Louongo knew the only really important calls came at night. During normal business hours, it could wait. After the phone rang several times, he answered, irritated, "Louongo, what do ya want?"

"Mister Louongo, sorry to bother you. This is Matt Tomas. I just wanted to thank you for everything you've done. I'll be sending your payment today. It's just great the way you helped us out."

Testimonials weren't common for the Louongo Law Firm. And he wasn't sure why Tomas was so happy. "Glad to be of service," he replied without conviction. "Exactly what sort of bullshit did I do to make you so fuckin' happy?" Might as well get to the point.

"They just gave me the reward. It's going to change our lives. We've decided to move to California and start over. Thank you so much."

Louongo hadn't known anything about a reward. "Glad I could help. Now, how much was this reward, again?"

"A hundred thousand dollars. It's from that bank somewhere overseas. I guess those certificates were real. Anyway, it's fantastic, and I just wanted to let you know how much we appreciate all you did."

Fuck. A reward. How did he miss that? "Great, Matt. I'm glad everything worked out." Maybe as some kind of joke the FBI told Tomas he'd handled the reward deal and didn't want a cut. At any rate, somebody was messin' with him. But, what the hell. He didn't need money. He had fame.

Still, this whole part of the country was starting to get on his nerves. He gave serious thought to going back to Jersey. At least he understood how people talked there, and his law license restriction period was about up. Maybe it was time to go home. Fuck Oklahoma.

Blackman had been on the phone most of the day with a real attorney in Dallas with a firm that helped him set up money stashes in several cooperative countries. The guy said the feds were bastards and he could help. If nothing else, Blackman liked his attitude. He told Blackman to turn himself in the next morning, and he'd be there to get him out. Once that was over, they could talk about more permanent ideas.

He felt better already. He fixed another drink—he'd already had several—and leaned back in his leather chair. He was thinking about getting out of the country—maybe even using the election as a kind of cover to get away from the asshole feds. As the alcohol eased his mind, he actually started to grin. He'd beat this shit.

He heard something, maybe one of the household staff. He sipped his drink.

"Fixin' to get shit-faced, Henry?"

Blackman flinched, startled only a moment. "Well, well, look who's here. My old asshole pal who's stabbed me in the back." Blackman was almost shouting while he got up.

Ed Black had a pistol out. "Be best, Henry, if you sat back down."

They glared at each other a few seconds.

Blackman plopped into his chair, scowling, not looking at

all afraid. "I can't believe you hate me so much you'd rat to the feds. Does that make you feel better—to fuck up *my* life?" He kept his voice low. It occurred to him there could be no reason for Ed to be here except to kill him. He started calculating.

"I'd be most pleased to fuck up your life. But talking to the feds? That's not something I'd do, even to get back at you for all you've done to me. What am I supposed to have told them, anyway?"

"They're charging me with tax and stock fraud. Who else would know all that shit?"

Black snickered. "You've really gotten dumb. The people who know about all that shit are the poor slobs whose butts you've kicked for years. The accountants and attorneys you've yelled at and browbeat. I'd bet every last one of those bastards decided you shouldn't be a senator and called the FBI or the IRS or the SEC, or whoever. And now the details, documents, facts, are all in the hands of the feds. But you, being the dumb shit you are, thought it was me. In case you've forgotten, I'm the guy they're looking for on a murder charge. What'd you think—I went to them and said, 'I can give you Blackman's head on a platter if you'll just let me off for murder?' Henry, all those street smarts you used to have are gone. Now you're just a pompous dictator who doesn't know or care how much people hate you. I can think of ten or so accountants you've treated like shit, and they all probably think it'd be just fine for you to be locked up for good. All the while, you're trying to act like a normal businessman, and of all things, you've got the nerve to run for office." He nodded meaningfully. "You've screwed up, big time."

Of course it was the accountants. They had all the damned

facts. He hadn't thought about that because it was just like Ed said—in his world they were barely people, just there to yell at anytime he heard bad news. The damned accountants. Besides, if Ed had wanted, he would've just killed him. He wouldn't blab to a fed. Blackman slumped. "Ed, all this success, power, the whole damn senate thing—I lost my mind. Of course it wasn't you. I don't know what I was thinking. Look—I've got money hidden all over. We just need to get out of the country, and we can live like kings," He leaned forward, trying to make a sale. "It'll be just like old times—we can drink all day; screw all the women we want. It'll be great. I need your help to get us out, but then everything'll be wonderful. Rich and free. We can find someplace, somewhere, maybe even *buy* the government. How about it, Ed?"

Ed wondered what had become of the tough, always-right guy he once knew. With all his success and fame, he'd shrunk into a bully, a weakling who needed other people to help him do anything. At one time, Henry Blackman would've taken charge and forced his will on anyone who stood in his way. Now he whined like an old woman, trying to get Ed to help him escape. He wasn't sure why he should feel sorry for Henry, but he did. The man who took no shit off anybody was now useless, except maybe for his money. But Ed didn't need money. He had a cabin deep in the Rockies with plenty to live on. He was going there to die. The thought gave him peace with all that had happened his entire miserable life.

He shot Henry Blackman twice in the head.

OK Journal

My View—Tommy Jacks

T.D. McFadden wasn't perfect.

Just ask his ex-wife. He left her for the same will-o'-the-wisp promises too many men see in women besides the ones they'd promised to have and to hold until death did part them.

Just ask the woman he left his wife for. Even after everything he gave up, including the peace of mind that comes with personal integrity, fidelity and run-of-the-mill uprightness, she had nothing good to say about him. When he needed her most, she wanted nothing to do with him.

Just ask Loretta Lynch, his former office manager and the woman who admitted she walked up to him while he puttered in the humble yard of his last refuge in east Oklahoma County, raised a pistol, shot him in the head, and left him dead.

If you want to get judgmental, T.D. McFadden messed up about as badly as possible. He'd worked too closely with men who used him like a shop rag, trafficking killer heroin under cover of his used-car businesses. He didn't keep a close eye on what they did or how they did it because he was too busy trying too hard to keep the hard-to-please girlfriend who'd broken his home.

But Lynch saw it all and where it was headed, which was the end of the job she needed to keep her husband alive. He was dying of cancer and needed cruelly expensive treatments. McFadden's mistakes cost her the job, and her husband died an agonizing death.

Still, none of that means Mc-Fadden was a bad man. He was a good man, and a good Democrat, and well regarded. He didn't mind not getting the headlines. He never cared about being more than what he was at his best: a businessman, a member of the state House of Representatives and holder of committee chairmanships.

And he gave people chances. Some, like Lynch and my father, needed them badly. Raymond Jacks was just out of state prison, freed after politically inspired convictions that put him there fell apart under investigation. Even after he and McFadden had been on opposite sides of some matters, T.D. gave him his first job on the outside, and it's been onward and upward since.

But he also gave chances to the Harris brothers, who are two of the men who used his businesses as Trojan Horses to cast in heroin that sent addicts to the Oklahoma City morgue.

McFadden was a good man, but he made bad choices. None of that means he deserved what happened to him. Nor does it mean Lynch should have gotten any sentence other that what was given her—the kind that fits the situation of someone whose mind also suffered in the name of love. ✿

28
SHOCKING NEWS

The capitol press room phone rang.

"Hey, Tommy—Dick Fitzgerald. Big story. Thought I should give you a heads-up. Henry Blackman's body was found this morning by one of his housekeepers. Shot twice in the head, I'm told. My police contacts say, on the QT, they've put out an APB for Ed Black, Connex's old head of security. They were already looking for him because of the tank inspector's murder, and they think he killed Blackman, too."

Tommy sat, shocked. Sure, murders happened, even to rich people. But a candidate in the U.S. Senate race, in the final days of the campaign? That was something no one would've guessed. "Think they'll catch him?"

"Nah. The real cops, street cops, told me the guy was likely out of the state before the body was found. The whole hoopla is just to cover their asses. A lot of these cops know Ed Black, and they always thought he was more criminal than corporate security man. They suspect he came back to Tulsa just to kill his old boss for revenge or whatever. And I have no details on this, but I've been told Blackman was supposed to turn himself in this morning to U.S. marshals on charges of tax and stock fraud. Obviously, he didn't make that appointment."

Tommy called June at the *Journal.*

"Yep, we're just getting that from UPI. Is this whole state going nuts? Assassination attempt of a senate candidate at a public debate, and now another candidate gets murdered in his home."

"I think Blackman was killed because of legal and business crap. Fillmore's shooting was just political craziness. There's just too much hatred in the world right now." Tommy began not to feel well. He asked June to call if anything major came up. He turned on the little TV.

Oklahoma AM was on, and the segment was a co-host of Tracy's talking about protecting plants for the first freeze of the year expected that weekend. He marveled at how important protecting plants could sound. High urgency infected everyone's remarks on the matter. *This is what we should worry about*, he thought, *not dead candidates.*

A news bulletin broke in. Tracy was on camera. "We've just received news that U.S. Senate candidate Henry Blackman has been killed. His body was discovered in his home early this morning, and police say he'd been shot. They've begun a manhunt for Ed Black, once head of security of Connex, Blackman's former company. What this will mean to the senate race and who, if anyone, might replace Blackman, isn't yet clear. We'll have more later, so stay tuned."

Vince popped in. "I just heard." He clapped his hands to his head. "What happens now?"

"Well, hello to you, too. Yeah." Tommy tried to think his way through it out loud. "There's not enough time to change the ballot. So Fillmore and Blackman have to be on it. The governor can postpone the election, but that won't happen—too big a mess. If Blackman wins, since he's dead, Bud would appoint someone to fill in until a special election." He thought a moment. "So, Bud might announce before the election who he'd appoint if Blackman won, which might help if enough people like who that is. But who? Besides, I bet revelations will come out about the charges against Blackman, and he'll lose most of the support he had. Could be split between Olsen and Fillmore."

"Better get this election over while there's still someone left standing." Vince was not half kidding.

"Mister Jacks, Taylor Albright is here to see you. He didn't have an appointment."

"Great. Show him up." Ray Jacks smiled at the thought of seeing Taylor. He considered him one of his best friends, especially after he'd helped him escape the hell of prison on unjust charges. He'd always owe Taylor more than he could repay.

Taylor scanned the office. "Wow, quite a layout you have here. You must be pretty damn important."

"I get a big office so they don't have to pay me so much. Come in, great to see ya. You're not here looking for a last-minute endorsement of Fillmore, are you?" Ray was smiling.

He grinned hopefully. "If Robbie wanted to, Howard sure wouldn't object."

"Unfortunately, Robbie still thinks the *Sun* should pass on this one. How's Howard doing?"

"Better. He's still in ICU, but no longer in a coma. The doctors say he was lucky—missed his heart by less than an inch. He'll probably never have full function of his right shoulder. But, no other permanent damage. So now it's about recovery, and they don't know how long. But he's healthy. He'll make it."

"That's great. I know it's not likely, but I hope he wins. Although, after all that's happened, he might just as soon lose."

"Haven't had a chance to talk to him, but I'd guess he'll be fine with whatever. He really is the best man for the job." There was sadness in Albright's voice. "Hey, no reason to be down. I stopped by to say so long again. Headed back to New York. Flying out this afternoon."

"Maybe we'll see each other sooner than you think. No one knows this yet, including Tommy, but Tracy was offered a hosting job for a new morning show on ABC in New York. It's the big time, and she can't turn it down. It wasn't a hundred percent for sure until just this morning. So, looks like we'll be neighbors." Ray was happy, sad, confused, anxious, scared, and several other emotions all tied up inside. He dreaded telling Tommy.

"Hey, how about that? Great for her, what an accomplishment. I know a bunch of people at ABC if she runs into any trouble. Plus, I know the perfect real estate person to help you find a place. You and Tracy in New York City, that's just great."

Governor Bud Evans's office released a short announcement praising the memory of Henry Blackman and offering condolences to his family for their loss, a part later corrected after it appeared no one knew of anyone who would claim him as family. The statement added that if Blackman won, Rick Butler, the current Republican senator, would remain in office until a special election a year later.

Sources in Senator Butler's office told reporters off the record about the loud exchange between him and the governor, in which Butler described Washington, D.C. as a "hell hole." The governor, according to those sources, reassured Butler there was almost no chance Blackman's corpse would win.

"Dad just called and wants us over for dinner. Said there was something he and Tracy wanted to tell us. Are you available?" Tommy's world always seemed better when he talked to Patsy.

"Sure, I'll swing by and pick you up. Know what it's about?"

"Nope, no idea. Maybe new furniture they're thinking of buying or something."

Tommy was stunned. "Moving to New York City?!" Patsy was crying and hugging Tracy.

"I know it feels like a big deal," Ray explained. "But we'll still see each other a lot. You and Patsy can come visit us maybe every few months, and we'll be back here now and again. I mean, we go weeks now without seeing one another. Now, we'll just be in a different town—that's all."

Tommy realized he sounded like an abandoned child and he was ruining the moment. "Wow, I guess it's just a shock. But it's wonderful. What a great opportunity for you, Tracy— you're going to be a huge success on national TV. You'll be famous." The enthusiasm wasn't real yet, but it was getting there.

Tracy smiled. "It's okay to feel like you do. I've had a few days to think, and I'm still not completely sure it's the right thing to do. But this is the big time, and at my age it's almost a miracle. I just can't turn it down. Maybe I'll flop, and it's a year away and we're back—I have no idea. But I have to try." Tracy was starting to cry.

"Of course you do. It's going to be wonderful. I'll have a famous mom." Tommy hugged her.

"We want you and Patsy to move into the house," Ray interjected. "No objections. We aren't going to sell because, like Tracy said, who knows what will happen? So, there's no reason for it to sit vacant. You can live here at no cost and put your money into savings—and you'd be doing us a favor by babysitting the place." Ray himself was unsure how he'd fit into the New York media world with a soon-to-be-famous wife supporting him. He hadn't said much to Tracy because everything was happening so fast. But he didn't feel that comfortable.

Despite numerous sightings of Ed Black from California to Florida, nothing panned out. Blackman was only a candidate for the senate, but still, there was a federal law against shooting such people. The FBI added Ed to their Ten Most Wanted list, joining the most dangerous, despicable criminals in the nation. At last, Ed was somebody.

OK Journal

My View—Tommy Jacks

Howard Fillmore was shot for political reasons. His attacker, not long before he drew and fired, made sure everyone in hearing range understood that.

Fillmore's alive and conscious again. However, with appalling and dispiriting suddenness, his Republican opponent, Henry Blackman, isn't. Someone came into Blackman's home in Tulsa yesterday, without being seen, and killed him. If you're a fan of grisly details, you can find them elsewhere in today's paper. We'll just note that among those details is an absence of a clear motive.

Sources also say Blackman's body was found in such a way as to suggest he'd been sitting at point-blank range, facing his killer. That makes it reasonable to think he might have known who it was. And whoever that was seemed to know the way in and out of Blackman's house without being noticed. Also, no reports say anything was taken from Blackman or his house.

And while we're being cold about it, we'll shift the scene to the capitol, where Gov. Bud Evans, a Republican like Blackman, is forced to weigh and measure bitter options. At least one matter is beyond his responsibility. It's too late to remove anyone's name from the ballot. Still, it's easy to see how that can create more problems than it solves, e.g., what if Blackman wins?

If that happens, Evans will have to appoint someone to the seat to serve in his place, at least until another special election can be held for the remainder of the term.

Rick Butler, who served the remainder of Bruce Knight's term, has not been reticent about letting anyone know he's more than ready to come back to Oklahoma, put up his feet, and retire from public life.

Politics in Oklahoma has always been interesting. But everyone who's been watching it for any length of time preferred the days when it was interesting without being so deadly or complex.

29
THE ELECTION

Election day morning was glorious, with a bright blue sky, no clouds, no wind, and a slight chill in the air. It was a good day to vote, or not. And it was a good day to be alive.

Reverend Olsen came to his local polling place, which happened to be his church, bright and early with his usual entourage. Many people had commented on how subdued he'd been since the incident in Stillwater. He had only attended a couple of campaign events in the meantime and seemed withdrawn, even avoiding reporters. After he voted, he stepped toward several microphones set up by the press.

"We're blessed to have such a wonderful day to fulfill our civic duty. God's sure blessed the people today. I haven't commented on the killing of Henry Blackman because I think what happened to Mister Blackman was because of his sins. It saddens me that so many people seem to take to violence as a solution to anything. It's always wrong. We've had great tragedies just in this one campaign. Two people shot—it saddens my soul that such a great country and a great state have turned their backs on God, and now he must punish these people. The wrath of God isn't something we should take lightly. We must return our country to its core beliefs and respect the Almighty, or we're all doomed. If you haven't voted today, remember I'm the only candidate who's been chosen by God to lead this country. You only have one choice. Thank you, and God bless you."

The Reverend Olsen headed to his limo. Most of the reporters stood in silence.

Vince called to tell Tommy about it from a pay phone. "Sure not a smart political move, but Olsen says what he thinks."

"Can't believe it's a good thing to say Blackman died because he was a sinner, even if he was. Before Olsen was a candidate, I would've said stating that you were God's choice for any particular elected office wasn't a good idea. But lately I don't think I have a good handle on what voters think. I guess we'll find out tonight if it means anything." The whole thing had turned into a nightmare. Everyone he talked to wanted it over with.

"I guess. Something about Olsen doesn't seem right, though. He seemed almost in a trance. That booming voice of his was pretty much gone. He was being led around by his groupies, like there's something wrong." Vince, besides being good with facts, was a keen observer of people.

"Having somebody run at him with a gun and fire shots that just miss—maybe he's dealing with shock."

Across town, TV cameras were allowed into the ward to record Fillmore handing his absentee ballot to one of his aides. He sat propped up in bed and made a gallant effort to smile, although even a casual observer saw he wanted it to be over. The reporters and their crews hurried and left as if realizing they were intruding, even if asked, on a badly injured man who needed time to heal. It might've been smarter not to have shown how damaged Fillmore was.

The good weather and the attention drawn by a campaign that included an attempted assassination of one candidate, the murder of another charged with massive fraud, and a televangelist running as the God Party, led to a high turnout. TV stations had reporters out doing exit polling, but any pattern eluded them. Some voters seemed upset about Olsen's statement that morning. Others insisted he was exactly right, that the country was falling apart. Some said they'd be concerned about Fillmore's health if he won. No one mentioned Blackman.

The polls closed. Fillmore's and Olsen's campaigns canceled their watch parties. Olsen's spokesperson said the reverend was tired after a long campaign and didn't want to encourage people to consume alcohol. Fillmore's spokesperson said it was because the candidate was in the hospital and the campaign was too short on funds. The only people who really cared were in the news media. Now they had no place to be or to consume free booze.

Patsy and Tommy went to his parents' house to watch results. Tracy was working, hoping for a short night.

Results began to come in.

Tommy came back from the kitchen. "How's it looking?"

"Looks like Olsen and Fillmore are tied with around forty percent each, with the rest going to Blackman and that Workers Party guy. Most results are from urban areas, and I'm not sure what that means. I don't think anyone knows how the rural areas will vote. But my guess is Olsen will get more votes out there than Fillmore." Ray had a lot of experience on how to predict early returns, but it had been a while, and this was different.

Patsy was curious but wanted it over just like most people. "The numbers look like they're coming in pretty fast. Maybe we'll know soon."

Some hours later, the anchorman cleared his throat. "We're getting new numbers. We're approaching ninety-two percent of the precincts reporting. The three major candidates are Blackman with seventeen percent, Olsen with forty-one percent, and Fillmore, thirty-eight percent. The remaining precincts are all rural around the Tulsa area, which should look good for Olsen."

"Looks like Olsen wins." Tommy told himself he really didn't care. But of course, he did.

"Yeah, three percentage points. Gonna be hard to make that up with only those precincts still out." Ray sounded tired.

Patsy was asleep, curled up in a big stuffed chair and covered by a blanket.

"But look at the actual totals. Fillmore's really only twelve thousand votes behind, and some of those precincts he's talking about as being rural are really suburbs. So, I don't know that it's Olsen's yet." Tommy remarked.

The anchorman came on again. "We now have ninety-nine percent of the precincts reporting, and we're declaring a winner. Olsen takes thirty-nine percent of the vote and Fillmore gets forty percent. Democrat Howard Fillmore has won the U.S. Senate seat, beating out independent Robert S. Olsen."

Analysis of the outcome would go on for months, but early reporting indicated Olsen had actually lost big in rural areas around Tulsa once thought to be his precincts, particularly near his church and where he lived. The split between rural and urban voting patterns was surprisingly narrow; in fact, there was little to no difference. Blackman did best around the oil fields. Party affiliation was also a factor. Almost all support for Blackman was Republican. Olsen's was about sixty percent Republican and forty percent Democrat, and for Fillmore it was the opposite. Some of the wiser heads about Oklahoma politics said the more they looked at the results, the more confusing they were.

The Olsen campaign released a short announcement stating the reverend was sorry he lost and wished Fillmore good health. The reverend personally hadn't made a public statement since election day. Rumors spread that he had suffered some kind of mental breakdown. A spokesperson responded to condemn such rumors as "totally false."

The Fillmore camp also released a short announcement saying Fillmore was grateful for everyone's support and as soon as his health allowed, he would address the public and lay out a detailed plan for moving forward. Rumors spread about him, too, that he had suffered physical damage that would take months, if not years, to heal. His spokesperson declined comment.

A week after the election, Howard Fillmore released a statement:

> *"It is with tremendous regret that I must resign from my recently elected position as U.S. Senator. My doctors advise me that I would be putting my life at risk if I traveled, especially flying. I don't see how I can perform the required duties of this office with my current medical problems. I'm sorry this has happened. It would have been the greatest honor of my life to have served as your Senator."*

This announcement created a whirlwind of speculation about legal and political implications. Camps formed and chose sides based on political party or religious grounds. People began picking sides. The governor had to clear things up, even if his decision could be challenged in court. He could declare the election void and call for a new one as soon as possible. Or he could take the position that the election was official, accept Fillmore's resignation, and appoint a replacement to serve until a special election could be held.

Howard Fillmore was a Democrat. The governor, Bud Evans, was a Republican. There were national implications related to the party make-up of the senate. The governor's phone hadn't stopped ringing for days.

"Hello, Tommy."

"Governor. What are you doing up here?" Tommy hadn't expected a visit from Bud Evans to the press room.

"Is it not allowed?" He seemed truly concerned.

"Oh. As far as I know, you can go anywhere you want."

Tommy chuckled nervously.

Evans took a chair across the desk and cleared his throat. "I guess you know about my dilemma?"

"Yes sir, I've heard a little about it."

"What do you think?"

"Me?"

"Yeah. What would you do?"

Tommy sat quietly for a bit. "Whatever you do, someone's going to be mad and probably take you to court. But still, you should do what you think's best for the state and the country—not the party. The Democrats think they won, but they already have control of the Senate, and one seat's not going to change anything. So you should pick someone who would do the best job, regardless of party."

"That makes sense. I should tell you I talked to Olsen yesterday. He told me he didn't want the job, that he was being treated for anxiety." Evans shrugged. "Who would you recommend?"

Tommy looked him in the eye. "You, sir."

At the end of the day, the governor called a press conference.

"I know you hate this, but I won't be taking questions today. The purpose of this gathering is to announce my decision regarding the U.S. Senate election. After the dust settles, I'll hold a real news conference and take questions at that time. First, I want to congratulate the voters of Oklahoma. It was a strange and frightening election season, but the voters stuck with it and made their decision known. I respect your decision, and I would've been pleased to have Howard Fillmore represent our state, even if we're in different parties. Also, let me say I respect Doctor Fillmore's difficult decision that he wasn't physically able to perform the duties of office. Also, you should know I've talked to Reverend Olsen, and he's given me permission to relay to you that he also suffers after that tragic shooting and believes he needs to heal further and doesn't feel fit to take the job. Reverend Olsen's a good man, more than just a religious man, and he cares about all of us." He took a deep breath. "There's no easy way for me to break this news, but I've decided to appoint myself to the U.S. Senate seat just elected, but not before I direct that a special election be held in eighteen months. I chose eighteen months because I think we need some healing time ourselves. And that'll allow all can-didates time to make their cases. I will not take part in that special election. Thank you." He left to a cacophony of shouted questions from the reporters.

OK Journal

My View—Tommy Jacks

And in the end the U.S. Senate seat that seven candidates seemed to want more than a year ago turned out to be a job nobody—at least, nobody alive who could do it without risk to health—really wants. But somehow, it works out.

Bruce Knight checked out with more than three years left to go. He shot a deranged, heroin-pushing doctor who'd killed his wife, and then himself. Rick Butler, governor at the time, appointed himself to the remainder of Knight's term and almost immediately regretted it. We've been told his furniture's already back in his house in Oklahoma City, bolted to the floor.

Howard Fillmore, the president of Oklahoma Corinthian College who won the seat back for the Democrats, wanted it, but not enough to die for it. He listened to doctors who told him and showed him he might not make it to the end of next year, let alone six, if he took the job and suffered the rigors it demands.

The Rev. Robert S. Olsen, who we promise on the Bible we'll never make fun of again, could have laid claim to it after Fillmore made his announcement. But he demurred for reasons I, first among all, completely understand. Being in the line of fire as he was that fateful night in Stillwater several weeks ago changes a man. It takes courage to know oneself that well, and to bear other people in mind while considering what to do. Olsen did that for himself and for us. He deserves our respect.

It's fair to assume Henry Blackman might still have wanted it, but someone else presumed to intervene, also with bullets.

Even Gov. Bud Evans, who soon will head to Washington to tag the grateful Butler out, has made it clear he doesn't plan to stay longer than he has to.

It's worth noting how ironic that has come to seem. Even if he's keeping the seat Republican, and therefore gives the Democratic Party of Oklahoma reason to consider raising heck about that, its leaders, and other interested political types and organizations, backed down to bide their time for a reason they all could agree on. We could do worse than to have Bud Evans as a senator, for any amount of time.

That will be about a year and a half, give or take. Evans was right when he said, in effect, that we all need at least that long to count our pieces and make decisions about what we want our next elections to be like. And we need time for people who consider running for election to such offices to give deep thought to the risks and demands of politics. And the rest of us need to ask ourselves what we can do—or maybe, not do—to keep a campaign like this from ever happening again. 🐾

30
LOVE AND MARRIAGE

"What would you do, Dad, if your Democratic candidate won an election but couldn't serve and the Republican governor appointed a Republican?" Tommy smiled like he knew the answer.

"Well, let's see. I guess I'd praise the governor for making a good choice."

"You expect me to believe that?"

"No."

"Where'd Tracy and Patsy go?"

"Shopping for something."

"Are you going to look for a job in New York?"

Ray frowned. "I guess. Not sure what that job would be, though. Can't imagine waiting around for Tracy to come home while I spend the day watching TV."

"Can Robbie help?"

"He kind of made a job for me that didn't require a lot of newspaper background. Probably won't find that situation in New York."

"There's always Albright. Bet he can find you something."

"I'm sure he'd try, but not too confident it'll generate any results. My best bet is just to take some time to look around and see what happens. If I say I want to do a particular thing, it might limit my chances. So, who knows? Does worry me, though. I don't want to become totally dependent on Tracy, and I sure don't want to be a distraction. Hey, New York's a big Democratic state. Maybe I could be an assistant to the party chairman or something." Ray grinned, but still looked worried. "Or maybe I just come back here and live with you and Patsy. What do ya think?"

Tommy cleared his throat. "I think I hope it all works out, Dad. You and Tracy need to stay together."

"What, is that a no? I can't come back and live with you and Patsy?"

"You know, you're not really very funny."

"Yes I am." He was.

"We're home. Where is everybody?" Tracy shouted out. "Here you are."

Ray and Tommy were in the same place as when she and Patsy had left.

"What's going on?" Tommy asked. "You seem excited."

"Yes, I am. Patsy said yes. Tommy, Patsy said yes. You're going to get married before we leave. Isn't that wonderful?" Tracy smiled hugely.

Tommy blinked. He wasn't sure where Patsy was. And he felt confused and a bit embarrassed. "Patsy said yes to you. Shouldn't she say yes to me?"

"Yes. I should've said yes to you. So, the answer's yes!" Patsy appeared in the doorway with a childlike smile.

Tommy tried not to look or sound as overcome as he felt. "This doesn't have anything to do with the house and now I'm rich, does it?"

Tracy slugged him in the shoulder.

Patsy giggled. "No, it's not the house. You've grown up.

You're no longer a baby. So, let's get married."

"I think that's a good idea." Ray added his approval.

Even a simple wedding at home took time to put together. They had to get a license, a blood test, buy a wedding dress, arrange for someone legal to do the ceremony, invite guests, arrange for food, and a lot more. Tracy was the main organizer and seemed to have a wonderful time handling the various duties. The ceremony would be at her and Ray's house, soon to be Tommy and Patsy's. They wanted a limited number of guests, but making the list was one of the major tangles. "Who do you not invite?" was a topic almost every day.

The day of the wedding arrived. Tommy was nervous. Patsy was beautiful, jittery, and weepy. Taylor Albright flew in from New York. Louongo stayed in the back, looking very out of place, which he was. Bart didn't make it—something about not feeling comfortable around a bunch of important people. Bill Anderson, June, and Fred came from the paper, as did Vince and his wife, along with Patsy's parents, her uncle Larry Alexander, Larry Lopez, Robbie Gilmore from the *Sun*, and performing the service, Governor, soon to be Senator, Bud Evans.

He performed the ceremony perfectly and pronounced Tommy Jacks and Patricia White husband and wife. Tommy kissed Patsy and their guests applauded.

"A toast to my wonderful son and his beautiful wife. Please, Tommy and Patsy, always be good to one another and treasure the joy of love and companionship you'll have in your marriage. Tracy and I admire you both. You're good people who deserve a great life full of happiness. To Tommy and Patsy."

Ray teared up and hugged Tracy.

Tommy pulled Tracy aside. "This would've never happened without you. You're the best mom anyone could have. Thank you." Tracy, in tears, embraced him.

"Well, what now, Tommy?" Albright was always nosy.

Good question, Tommy thought. He had no idea. Maybe keep writing for the *Journal,* or maybe not. "I wanted to change things, make the world a better place. I wanted to be a muckraker. I'm not there yet. But I have some ideas."

EPILOGUE

Joe Louongo. Joe returned to New Jersey and flourished. He realized in a flash that he had been a fish out of water in fuckin' Okie land, but he was just another "guy" in Jersey. After bureaucratic snafus were settled, his law license was reinstated. He soon had a thriving practice and became the darling of the Newark media. That led to his running for the State Assembly and winning. Although the job of assemblyman was technically part-time, Joe spent a lot of time, some required and some not, in Trenton and again became a media star. He continued to practice law with a client list mostly of politicians. His vast experience in dealing with hardened criminals seemed a natural fit. People began to talk of him running for governor.

Taylor Albright. Taylor once again returned to the comforts of the Big Apple to lick his political wounds. Ignoring a hint of self-doubt, he wrote a novel titled *Adventures in Okanova,* a fictional account of a nation/state somewhere in Central America and it's amazing, screwed-up political system. It was a parody of everything he'd witnessed during his ventures into the heartland. It became a national best-seller, although sales in the Bible belt were limited by his generous use of foul language. He has been laughing a lot since.

William "Bill" Anderson. Recognizing the inevitable, Bill turned off the money spigot to the *OK Journal.* Within six months, it shut down. He felt badly that so many good people lost their jobs during a very difficult time in the news business, but he was certain he had no choice—sometimes you lose, and sometimes you win, and he had won a lot. He withdrew to his ranch and the horses he loved.

Robert "Robbie" Gilmore. While the newspaper business was not the cash cow it was in the "good old days," the closing of the *OK Journal* was good for the *Oklahoma Sun*. Robbie experienced new success and felt emboldened to venture beyond TV and newspapers. His wealth and his family's wealth grew. Given new responsibility for all of his prosperous business ventures, he considered selling the *Sun*. He knew J.H. would turn over in his grave, but he was ready to move on from the legacy of his tyrant father and be his own man at last.

Bud Evans. Nothing prepared Bud Evans for the meanness of Washington D.C. He'd heard the stories, but to see it in action, close-up, dispirited him. With some effort, he held on to his core belief that people were basically good, even if all evidence he saw daily proved otherwise. His goodness and penchant for hard work made him stick out like a different species. After fulfilment of his short-term commitment as a senator, he was ready to head home and do anything other than politics. He had discussions with Doctor Howard Fillmore about teaching at his school near Enid, which appealed to him. In another twist of fate, his reputation as a "good" man caught the attention of the current Republican president, who asked him to join his cabinet as Secretary of the Interior. The Department of Interior meant something to Evans. It was exactly what he wanted to do, but he wanted to be able to do it right and was not sure about the president. He reluctantly took the job and became the only member of the administration not considered a political hack. With his national reputation for integrity and honesty, he considered running for president.

Tracy Clark Jacks. She became an immediate hit and the "next new thing" on network television. Her looks, charm, and smarts made her stand out. Not being sure whether she even wanted to be in New York made her aggressive, so she did things her way. The audience fell in love. She was considered as an anchor for the nightly news show—not something a woman had ever done up to then. Although money and fame should make a person happy, she wasn't. Rather, she longed to be left alone, to move back to Oklahoma and hide. But she mostly stayed quiet about her feelings and smiled. At first, she and Ray took part in the ongoing, never-ending social activities made available, and on occasion demanded, by her new fame. Ray tried to fit in, but both soon tired of the effort. She knew the fame would soon fade. Most of their free time now was spent home alone, dressed in sweats, watching TV, and calling Tommy and Patsy.

Raymond "Ray" Jacks. Ray considered New York hectic and noisy. He found some freelance work with Albright's help, but it didn't last. With Tracy's massive success, money was not a concern. He soon fell into being a man-wife, his life centered around hers. At first, it felt wrong, but he adapted. He soon became a regular at the neighborhood bar on the ground floor of their building, visiting around lunchtime for a few beers and lots of sports talk, political gossip, and a few celebrity rumors thrown in. Tracy got home early in the afternoon most days, but of course, she had to be gone very early in the morning for the show. Ray would have dinner ready by the time she got home, and they would spend time together, doing mostly nothing. He didn't feel productive, but it was a life. He loved his wife, so he didn't complain. They became two people not enjoying their lives in amazing luxury.

Patsy White Jacks. Patsy was a new-age woman, but comfortable being a wife. She quit her job with her uncle and became active in community matters. She loved organizing things, and although she was one of the youngest women in her neighborhood, she soon became the chairwoman, president, leader, or go-to person for almost everything. She had the energy for it, and everyone loved her. Tommy turned one of the bedrooms into an office and spent considerable time at home writing. But anytime he stuck his head out to see what Patsy was doing, she was gone. He felt amazed by her energy and interest in every cause under the sun. Patsy talked to Tracy at least twice a week and knew, despite all her success, that she was unhappy. Patsy was not going to let that happen to her and Tommy. She determined that even if he had the talent to be a national success, they would stay in Oklahoma and be happy, not rich. She was soon pregnant. She told Tommy she wanted three kids. He nodded in agreement but seemed confused. It was clear to anyone who paid attention that Patsy was in charge.

Tommy Jacks. The shutting down of the *OK Journal* was like a death in the family. He mourned for weeks. It was more than a job—it was who he was. After several weeks, he got a call from Robbie Gilmore. The *Oklahoma Sun* offered him a job very similar to what he had been doing for the *Journal*: a two-to-three-times-a-week column focused on politics, but at almost twice the money. Tommy hadn't known he'd been so underpaid before. He, of course, consulted with Patsy, his dad, and Tracy, and all said, "Take it and continue doing what you're doing." That included the television segments for the Gilmore-owned station. But he didn't feel sure about it. The idea of bigger things was still in his head, even if he wasn't sure what those things were. Should he go to New York and take a chance? He thought about Patsy and the family they would soon have and made the decision to stay home and fight the battles in his own back yard. Tommy had been tamed, for the time being. Most heroes live quiet, unnoticed lives. He joined those ranks.

ABOUT THE AUTHORS

Ted Clifton has written mystery novels which feature the settings of New Mexico and Oklahoma, places where Ted spent considerable time. One of his books, *The Bootlegger's Legacy*, won the IBPA Benjamin Franklin award and the CIPA EVVY award. Today Ted and his wife reside in Denver, Colorado, after many years living in the New Mexico desert.

Once a month, Ted sends his readers a newsletter with a little of everything in it: southwest US culture, be it art, recipes, or local sights; his thoughts on writing and reading; book recommendations; updates on his current writing projects; and from time-to-time a short story.

To sign up, visit TedClifton.com and either wait for the pop-up window, or scroll to the bottom of the page. Everybody who signs up receives a mystery gift, with Ted's compliments. You can also learn more about Ted and his latest books by visiting TedClifton.com or emailing him at ask@tedclifton.com.

Stanley Nelson lives in Oklahoma, and works for what is presently the only book publisher staffed and operated by a Native American tribe. His background includes several years in newspapers as an editor and columnist. He edits and supplies text for several of the publisher's titles, and authored *Toli: Chickasaw Stickball Then and Now*, winner of an IBPA 2017 Gold Medal for Regional Non-Fiction.

BOOKS BY TED CLIFTON

Available from popular booksellers.

MURDER SO STRANGE

Muckraker Mystery #2

In an exclusive residential neighborhood, a U.S. Senator's wife has died. Tommy Jacks and his fellow journalists don't believe the police chief's story blaming it on natural causes. It has the smell of a crime. So begins a new journey set in the 1960s involving numerous dead bodies, high-tension political intrigue, police corruption, the drug underworld and unsavory hidden pasts. Tommy has a lot to write about in his My View political column.

Only in his second year as a political columnist, he finds new romance and emotional healing among a chaotic mixture of characters, from his new mother and his recently out-of-jail father to his acerbic journalistic mentor and antagonist and a foul-mouthed lawyer of questionable ethics, all wrapped inside the saga of two competing daily newspapers still at war.

Lurking in the shadows is the powerful and corrupt police chief, who seems to think it might be best if Mister Jacks, even so young, was dead.

Murder So Strange continues the 1960s saga of Tommy Jacks: Muckraker.

MURDER SO FINAL

Muckraker Mystery #3

Tommy Jacks, reporter, encounters new love and old threats while covering one of the most brutal U.S. Senate races in history. With a massive oil fire threatening the city of Tulsa, three candidates face off: a ruthless oil baron, an idealist college professor, and a reverend running under the God Party. When the race suddenly turns deadly, the winner may be the last man standing.

The final book in the Muckraker trilogy, Murder So Final brings to a close the stories of Louongo, Albright, Robbie Gilmore, Tracy and Ray Jacks, and Tommy himself.

DOG GONE LIES

Pacheco & Chino Mysteries #1

Sheriff Ray Pacheco returns from his introduction in The Bootlegger's Legacy to start a new chapter as a private investigator, along with his partners: Tyee Chino, often-drunk Apache fishing guide, and Big Jack, bait shop owner and philosopher.

The trio are pulled into a mystery immediately when an abandoned show dog appears at Ray's cabin and the dog's owner is reported missing. Ray and his team pursue leads that bring them into confrontations with the local sheriff, the mayor, and the FBI, while in the meantime two bodies are found—neither of which is the missing woman.

SKY HIGH STAKES

Pacheco & Chino Mysteries #2

Tired of spending his days fishing, Ray Pacheco takes on his second assignment with his partner Tyee Chino when the state Attorney General asks them to find out just what the hell is going on in Ruidoso, New Mexico. With the town's sheriff in the hospital with a mysterious illness, acting sheriff Martin Marino is running rough-shod over everyone around him.

What seems like a simple assignment becomes more complicated when Marino is found dead, shot at close range while sitting in his patrol car on Main Street. The suspects include most of the town, from Dick Franklin, manager of Ruidoso Downs racetrack, to bar owner Tito Annoya, to members of the local law enforcement.

At the same time, Ray has an uneasy feeling that the AG is withholding critical details about what exactly is going on in Ruidoso—and why the state was so slow to respond.

It all comes to a surprising conclusion with the involvement of a Spanish princess, a drug lord gone mad, and a few other lowlifes . . . and leaves Ray wondering if maybe fishing wasn't so boring after all.

FOUR CORNERS WAR

Pacheco & Chino Mysteries #3

Rejoin Ray Pacheco and Tyee Chino in their latest adventure unraveling a maze of misdeeds involving wealth, power, political corruption and Navajo warriors.

Farmington, New Mexico, located in the Four Corners area

where four states meet, is about to experience a level of crime and mayhem never seen before. The local sheriff has abandoned his post and taken old military equipment, including a tank, off to Colorado to prepare for the beginning of the end. Left behind is the body of his wife, who was having an affair with the richest man in town.

Money, sex and all known sins come into play in a small-town drama that will take Pacheco and Chino into a conflict that will involve many of the good citizens of Farmington and the nearby Navajo Nation.

SANTA FE MOJO

Vincent Malone Book 1

Vincent Malone was once a hot-shot Dallas attorney, but booze and bad judgement brought that and his marriage to an abrupt end. Battling gout and barely paying the bills as a legal investigator, Malone's unreliability costs him his last client.

Heading south with no idea of what the future may hold, Malone takes a know-nothing job as a shuttle driver for a B&B in Santa Fe, where he meets the clients of a big-time LA sports agent. Gathered to celebrate their success, things go sour quickly when missing millions, sexual entanglements, and personal histories lead to murder.

Malone finds himself in the middle of a major murder case with the lead detective giving him the evil eye. Malone teams up with an aging gun-slinger attorney to find the real killer and clear an innocent man.

BLUE FLOWER RED THORNS

Vincent Malone Book 2

Vincent Malone, hot-shot attorney turned shuttle driver, finds himself in the middle of another murder case.

The international contemporary art scene has come to Santa Fe, New Mexico, and brought plenty of ego, feuds, and sexual entanglements along with it. Vincent's employer, the Blue Door inn, is hosting a big artist for her U.S. debut and nothing is going smoothly. The artist and gallery owner are threatening each other, and before long there is one dead body and plenty of suspects.

Malone dusts off his private investigator skills to solve this tangled mystery with an unusual cast of characters, plenty of false leads, and a surprise ending following many twists and turns.

FICTION NO MORE

Vincent Malone Book 3

A mystery author staying at the Blue Door Inn claims she is being followed. Vincent Malone volunteers to find out what is going on, and things quickly get complicated.

The author's first book is about a murder that took place forty years in the past, but the details are suspiciously specific. The victim's adult son would like to know how the author came by this information. Soon, a bullying sheriff and a wayward priest are involved, along with a priceless—and stolen—collection of Pueblo Indian artifacts.

When the situation turns deadly, Malone must find out

who committed the murder, and why. Past misdeeds long buried will come to light, and fiction will be separated from fact, as Malone pursues the truth.

THE BOOTLEGGER'S LEGACY

Prequel to the Pacheco & Chino mystery series.
When an old-time bootlegger dies and leaves his son Mike a cryptic letter hinting at millions in hidden cash, Mike and his friend Joe embark on a journey that takes them through three states and 50 years of history. What they find goes beyond money and transforms them both.

This is an action-packed adventure story that partially takes place in the early 1950s. It all starts with a key, embossed with the letters CB, and a cryptic reference to Deep Deuce, a neighborhood once filled with hot jazz and gangs of bootleggers. Out of those threads is woven a tapestry of history, romance, drama, and mystery; connecting two generations and two families in the adventure of a lifetime.

Winner of the IBPA Benjamin Frankling Digital Awards (2016 Silver Honoree).

> "The Bootlegger's Legacy takes the reader on a wild ride through Oklahoma's bootlegging history. It makes for a wonderful escape into a fascinating, dangerous, and strange world filled with characters your mother warned you about. Most readers will only ever interact with these types in make believe, but while the ride lasts it's a rollicking good time."
>
> —*Self-Publishing Review, 4 Stars*

"Although the mystery elements in this novel are certainly engaging enough to keep readers turning pages, it's Clifton's superb character development that makes this story a transformative journey of self-discovery. The noteworthy narrative also includes vivid backdrops, brisk pacing, and a meticulously researched, historically accurate account of the Prohibition era in Oklahoma and Texas. A tale with an authentic, immersive setting, inhabited by well-developed, endearing characters."

—Kirkus Reviews